Heavenly Bo

MW00935854

"Great Book!!"

"This book is wonderful! ...rarely can you find a book with such a good message that is written in our modern times. I loved reading it and would recommend it to everyone! Great characters and plot that keeps you interested. I really encourage you to get this book don't just consider it. DO IT!!"

Clancy Russell (Feb. 5th 2014)

"Rebecca really knows how to write soft, relatable stories and she has made Joelle into a sarcastic, easy going personality which brings adventure and humor to the plot.

Heavenly Bodyguards is a beautiful concept because it talks about love and hope. It makes you believe in angels and that there is someone out there taking care of you. It is due to this reason that Heavenly Bodyguards is bound to become a readers' favorite. But more than anything, the book is about how you can look at things differently if you simply believe in yourself. Heavenly Bodyguards – Trainee in action is definitely a book worth reading.

Serious Reading

"This book is amazing, and so is the author!!!"

"... The book has a really inspiring message, and we can all relate to the Book. I am looking forward for the 2 and 3 book to come out! I do recommend this book!!!"

Emily Dowdle (Feb. 5th 2014)

"This is a MUST READ!"

"I thoroughly enjoyed reading Heavenly Bodyguards.
The characters are down to earth and lovable, it is laced with humor
and wit to keep it interesting. Great story line. I love reading clean,
fun books. This book definitely falls into that category."

Carmen (Oct 23rd 2017)

"Creativity and Imagination = Captivating..."

"I was privileged to work on a few sections of "Heavenly
Bodyguards: Trainee in Action" with Rebecca. It is Ms. Lange's
creativity and imagination that made this book so captivating! The
descriptions of scenes will make the reader feel as if he/she is right
there. I loved the characters and found myself cheering them on.
Although I have not done any research, I doubt if there are very
many fiction books on "heavenly bodyguards," which makes this
book even more unique.

I loved this book and highly recommend it! Can't wait for the next
installment!"

Edwina E. Cowgill (March 13th 2016)

German Review:

"Das Leben aus Sicht unserer Schutzengel zu betrachten ist eine
super Idee. Sich vorzustellen, dass man in seinem Leben mehr
Schutz und Begleitung hat, als einem bewusst ist, empfinde ich als
tröstlich und aufbauend. Ich habe die Geschichte von Joelle, dem
Schutzengel in Ausbildung, wirklich gerne gelesen und freue mich
auf die Fortsetzung."

Heavenly Bodyguards- Trainee in Action

By

Rebecca Lange

More books by Rebecca Lange:

German Deliciousness

Coming soon:

Heavenly Bodyguards – Against all Evil

Heavenly Bodyguards – Hurtful Conspiracy

Author Rebecca Lange
Editing by Edwina Cowgill, Michele Reagan and Nicholas Cieslak

Book cover/ printing – by Createspace and Amazon

For more information about the author (or for finding out about other projects the author is working on), please visit her website at www.rebeccalange.weebly.com

First edition printing in paperbound 2013.
Second edition printing in paperbound 2018.

ISBN-13: 978-1985878105

ISBN-10: 1985878100

For my children and husband,
who so patiently let me write this story.

ACKNOWLEDGMENTS

Thanks goes to:

- my husband Nick who helped edit the book,
- my friend Michele also helping with the editing,
- my editor Edwina and all the work she put into it
- my Mom who herself has a talent for writing
- my children who were so patient while I created this wonderful unique story.

All of you are very special to me and
I will always be grateful
for your support and
understanding.

How this trilogy came about…

One day, early in the summer of 2012, my husband and I were on a date. During our conversation he suggested, out of the blue, that I write a book. Naturally I was stunned and asked him what made him suggest it. He told me it was something he felt I should try. He knew how much I love to write, and that I had created stories in my teenage years. Never in the world would I have thought to write something for the public to read.

But, for someone who likes challenges, a thought like this doesn't get planted into my head without me taking it to the next level. As soon as I decided to go for it, I knew I would have to come up with a good unique story. I needed something that wasn't out there yet, something fiction, but potentially true. It didn't take long (we were still on our date driving to our destination) before the thought of guardian angels entered my mind. I didn't know what to make of it at first. I kept thinking: "this can't be it", but I couldn't get rid of the thought.

So I went along with it. The fact that I finished all three books within a year shows me I picked the right story. I believe in life after death, and I've always wondered what happens to those who pass on. Well, why not think of them as guardian angels? Anything is possible, right? But even if it is possible, let's not get carried away. Heavenly Bodyguards is just a fictional story… or is it?
☺

Rebecca Lange

Contents

A Note from the Author:

When I wrote this book, I had no idea where this would lead me. I knew it was a unique story, but there was more to it than just words and ideas. I felt this was something I should write about.

Writing has been one of my biggest passions since my childhood. I always enjoyed creating stories, dreaming myself into characters, and leaving reality for a bit. The written word can make escaping into a fantasy world so much fun. I love when my imagination runs wild and creates something that didn't exist before.

Writing is my outlet and a way to communicate better. It isn't always easy for me to verbally say what I mean, but putting it on paper (or the computer/ iPad/ phone) makes such a difference.

I knew it was important not only to address "every-day-life-situations", but things that meant something. I wanted to share some of my beliefs and feelings so readers would understand where I was coming from. I am a very religious person, and love my Heavenly Father. He created us and is on the other side of the veil, waiting for us to return. He loves us and will love us no matter what we do and choose. He even loves those who choose to follow Satan. He might not like what we do or decide, but He will never stop loving us.

I want you to know that Heavenly Father is always there for us and He will never leave us. He will accept our choices because He wants us to have free agency, but He will never abandon us.

Heavenly Bodyguards – Trainee in Action is Part one of the Heavenly Bodyguards trilogy. It plays mostly in Scotland. This book is fiction, but I also shared some of my own experiences from when I lived in Scotland as a missionary for my church. Since I always try to stick to my own writing style and ideas, I thought it would be fun if I customized my writing to the setting of the story. That means the grammar is a mix of American- and British English. My story starts out in the US, but plays mostly in Scotland, so I adjusted the spelling and different words accordingly. I attached a small dictionary at the end of this book, to make it easier for everyone who doesn't know the different words between those two English-speaking accents.
<u>US-readers:</u> Don't be surprised if you find certain words spelled in a way you didn't expect. It isn't a grammar error, they really spell it like that in Britain.

This book addresses many issues and topics: loss through death, life after death, faith, love, trust, dishonesty, abuse, sexual harassment, kidnapping and several more.

We can only change things when we talk about it.
We can only change things when we are willing to listen.
We can only change things when we love others even if we disagree.

I truly hope you will enjoy this novel. Don't forget that you are loved by a loving Heavenly Father and He wants you to come back to Him. Happy reading!
Love,
Rebecca Lange

1. Dream or Reality?

Joelle watched as a decent size truck sped down the street. As the truck came closer, the driver saw a little girl run into the intersection. He tried to slow down, but moved too fast to stop in time. The loud screeching brakes startled everyone waiting for the traffic lights. People's eyes were glued to the fast moving vehicle, and the girl in the street.

The truck driver had plain terror written on his face as he tried to stop his truck. Men and women watched in horror as the accident unfolded and the truck came closer and closer. Many covered their faces with their hands to keep themselves from screaming in shock.

Without even thinking, Joelle jumped into the street. She grabbed the little girl, turned herself away from the truck so her body covered the child, and tried to get out of the way… unfortunately too late. The truck connected and both Joelle and the girl got knocked through the air with Joelle still holding the toddler to her body.

Joelle landed on her back and rolled to her side. She couldn't breathe and her whole body was in horrible pain.

The truck came to a standstill. The driver got out of the vehicle, kneeling by Joelle's side.

"SOMEONE CALL 911!" he shouted.

The toddler's mother hysterically screamed for her baby and kept pushing pedestrians out of the way to find her child.

In a few seconds Joelle saw her whole life flash by. She remembered everything leading up to the moment of the accident.

**

It had been one of those mornings. She was running late for class and was supposed to give her students an exam in just a few minutes. Joelle had been waiting at the last traffic light when the light turned red.

She had looked around trying to distract herself from the stress of being so late, when a man sneaked up to a woman on the other side of the street.

The woman held a screaming toddler by the hand as she waited for the light to change. The kid wanted to escape, but the mom didn't let go.

Joelle remembered how the man reached the woman. He grabbed her purse, but before he turned around, and make his escape, the woman noticed what he was doing.

She held her bag and hit him in the face while trying to get away. During the confusion, the woman's child broke free and sneaked around the crowd of people.

Others nearby came to the woman's aid, but the wanna-be-thief escaped. Not realizing where her daughter was, the mother turned in search of her child.

That was the moment when the toddler ran into the street and Joelle jumped in front to protect her from the truck.

**

Now they were both laying on the ground. Joelle's body tensed up in excruciating pain. She looked into the little girl's big blue eyes filled with shock and fright.

The child cried loudly, calling for her mom. The mother reached Joelle and took her screaming child from Joelle's bleeding arms.

"Don't move, help is coming right away," she told Joelle trying to sound as calm as possible.

Her whole body was shaking, from the shock and stress, as she thought about the whole incident. If it hadn't been for this young woman lying on the ground, her daughter would be dead now.

In desperate panic she checked her child to make sure she didn't get injured. Besides being in shock, the toddler seemed just fine.

The mother looked at Joelle who was in terrible shape. Tears ran down the woman's face as she knelt beside Joelle. Her daughter had calmed down now and clung to her mother.

"I am so sorry, Miss. I am so sorry." The mother muttered the words under her breath, holding her child with one arm and gently touching Joelle's forehead, brushing hair out of Joelle's face. Her sobbing became louder as she sensed how much agony Joelle felt.

The truck driver kept talking to Joelle and then someone else, in the crowd of people, shouted that the ambulance was on its way.

The pain became unbearable. Joelle gasped for air and blood ran from her mouth.

Two police cars reached the accident. One officer directed traffic, and the other two officers hurried over to where Joelle lay.

One guided the sobbing mother and her daughter to the side of the road, and the second officer knelt next to Joelle and spoke to her.

"Miss, can you hear me?" Joelle looked up and tried to nod, but it seemed as if her body shut down. She gazed around one last time, and everything around her became unclear. Then she noticed two women standing next to her, smiling at her with tears in their eyes.

Where did these women come from? She couldn't help thinking.

The police officer kept talking to her, but she didn't understand what he said. Traffic was building up and drivers passed the accident, hoping to get a glimpse of the scene.

The officer directing traffic, shouted at people to move them along as pedestrians tried to get closer to take pictures.

In a car, close to Joelle, someone listened to a familiar song. Right before her body was ready to give up, she heard the singer's voice: "What doesn't kill you makes you stronger….[1]"

Her thoughts went berserk. Someone in heaven either had the worst timing for trying to make those on earth feel better, or had the deepest blackest sense of humor ever. This was beyond ironic, but when she thought about it sometime later, she had to admit it was kind of funny. If she hadn't had been in such horrible pain, she would have laughed about it. This, however, was serious and not a joke but brutal reality. In agony she closed her eyes hoping this was just a bad dream. The next moment, the pain was gone.

She looked around and noticed that she stood next to her body now, looking at herself. The police officer kept talking to her and an ambulance and fire truck reached the accident now.

No! I'm not ready to die, she thought. *And I will not die right now!* She was determined to not let this happen

---

[1] Stronger, Kelly Clarkson, 2011

and tried to push her spirit back into the body, but it didn't work.

The two women still smiled.

How can they see me? No one else can. Who are they? Both gave her a kind and warm look.

Suddenly, a bright light appeared behind Joelle that pulled her backwards.

"We are your guardian angels, Jo. Your time is up, just follow the bright light."

"NOOOOOOOOO!" was all she wanted to scream, but she had no voice. She tried to stop herself from moving towards the light, but it seemed as if her spirit was being pulled to the light involuntarily.

Joelle looked back, and the two angels just waved at her until she was far away and didn't see them anymore.

She felt angry. *Are you freaking kidding me? I'm supposed to be giving an English test to my class, not walking through the clouds. Why can't someone just turn off this tractor beam that's pulling me along?*

It reminded her of the movie 'Star Wars' and how the spaceship of Luke Skywalker, and Han Solo, had been drawn into the Death Star. Just like them, there wasn't anything she could do to stop it.

The bright light opened to a wide space, and she saw herself walking toward a crowd of people dressed in white. As she looked down at herself, she noticed she was also dressed in a white dress somehow.

What happened to my clothes? This is getting creepy now, she thought.

Overwhelmed she looked around, when the next moment someone embraced her. Angrily she pushed away the young man who had just hugged her.

"Who are you and what gives you the right to step into my comfort zone?" Her voice was back and her eyes flashed as she put her hands on her hips.

He grinned at her. The sassy grin seemed familiar. She looked closer into his face and tried to remember.

Where have I seen this face before? Maybe in a picture, or movie? Then it clicked.

"No way! Grandpa? You are Grandpa aren't you?" He nodded with another grin. *That's why I have trouble remembering him, he's young now, not old the way I remember him.* He looked so handsome now, the same way he looked in his wedding picture.

Other people surrounded her and her grandfather, and seeing so many unfamiliar faces frustrated her even more. Until this point she believed, and hoped, she would wake up any minute and everything had just been a dream. That hope disappeared when she realized how real her surroundings were.

So this isn't a dream? I am dead?

Everyone seemed excited and happy to see her, but all she could think of was her disbelief of having left her earth life, family and friends.

Her grandfather took her in his arms again, and everyone talked to her at once. Her head was spinning, and she wasn't ready, or willing, to face this new reality.

Why am I here? Why does everything seem like a dream?

Her grandfather kept talking to her, but she couldn't hear what he said. Everything seemed so far away and unfamiliar.

Finally the crowd gave her space to breathe.

Bewildered, she looked at her grandfather and wanted to say something, but the words didn't come out.

He touched her arm.

"Jo, give it time. It will make sense soon, I promise." With a big smile he hugged her again. "It's so good to see you."

She tried to smile, but nothing worked right now.

Understanding how she felt, he left her alone, knowing she had to grasp her new reality first.

Letting herself fall to a sitting position on the ground, Joelle closed her eyes and opened them again. This wasn't a dream, she was in heaven, but she didn't want to be here. This was too soon. Something must have gone wrong. She was only thirty-five years old and had lots of stuff to do and finish. She wasn't ready to be dead.

Joelle jumped back to her feet and ran: running away from the crowd, running toward… she didn't even know where.

Her grandfather kept calling her, but she didn't want to listen. She had to get back to her body before it was too late.

"Jo, stop!"

"Sorry Grandpa," she yelled back, "this is wrong. I have to get back before I'm stuck here."

The next moment she stood next to her lifeless body, watching as people tried to revive her. She looked down at herself and the white dress was still there.

Her grandfather appeared, standing next to her, putting his arm around her shoulders.

"You've done what you had to do, Jo. This is real and you have to accept it."

Accept it? There's nothing to accept. This is a mistake. Many thoughts ran through her mind and she couldn't think clearly. *What about my parents? Mom is in a wheelchair and needs my help. Dad is in the early stages of Alzheimer's. He forgets where he is and has even gotten lost a few times. Are my older siblings going to take care of them or are they going to put them in a nursing home? Samuel, my oldest brother, lives in Boston with his family. My older sister, Jennifer, in Philadelphia. My parents don't want to move out of New York. What will happen now?*

And what about my two younger brothers? Michael is finishing up at Harvard Law School, and Brandon studies at NYU. I have been looking after them and supporting them financially. Samuel and Jennifer have

*never been supportive. They always do their own thing.
Sure, they expected Dad to pay for their school, but they
didn't do much for anyone else in return. Will they take
over now and help Michael and Brandon? Will they step
up and support the rest of the family?*

John looked at his granddaughter knowing what went
through her mind. He wanted her to be comfortable in
this new world, but she wasn't happy about her death
and kept holding on to her earth life.

He snapped his fingers and a moment later they
appeared back in heaven.

Joelle gave him an angry look. "Why are you taking
me away from my body? I don't want to be dead. I
shouldn't be here. Please take me back to earth so I can
enter my body again."

John shook his head.

"Sweetheart, your time is up. You are needed in our
world now."

"No. I don't want to be here, and I don't believe my
time is up either. I have so many things I want to do, and
have to do."

"Jo, come on, you can't change what happened. Your
family will be fine. Everything will work out."

He tried, once again, to get her out of her melancholy
state. Never in his years as an angel had he ever seen
anyone who so stubbornly held on to their human life.

Joelle couldn't move on. She had loved her life and
enjoyed working with cranky teenagers. She loved

making sarcastic remarks when the high-schoolers thought they were so clever and then making them laugh with her dry and sarcastic sense of humor. This couldn't be over.

It would make sense to be dead if she had been unhappy and hadn't been doing anything with her life. But she had been happy, and was always busy, loving every minute of it. Sure, she hadn't found Mr. Right yet, but she was only in her thirties. There was still time.

This whole situation didn't feel right. They must have mixed her up with someone else. This had to be a terrible mistake. Someone had pulled her out of life in the middle of her living it. This was not how she pictured her future.

I will not accept this, she thought. *I can't just die and leave everything to take care of itself. I mean how unorganized is this place? Someone messed up big time and they have to get me back to my human life.*

***

"Honey, you need to stop feeling so sorry for yourself and do what you're supposed to do," said a strange new voice.

Joelle threw her head back. A female angel, similar in age, stood in front of her with a smile on her face. Joelle had been so lost in her thoughts she didn't even notice the angel approach.

This angel had given Joelle a few minutes to settle down and let everything sink in, hoping this new young

11

angel would come around by herself. After realizing that nothing changed, the female angel concluded that Joelle needed a verbal nudge. And sure enough, it worked.

Joelle looked her straight in the eyes.

"How dare you talk to me like that? You don't even know me."

"Darling, I know more about you than you think. I know more about you than you do." She smiled at her, making Joelle even more frustrated and angry. Being called darling, or honey, was one of Jo's biggest pet-peeves.

John, her grandfather, smirked too. This was the granddaughter he knew and remembered: impulsive and explosive. Maybe now she was ready to accept her new surroundings.

Memories of his own life came to mind. Joelle had cared for him during the years he fought cancer. She had been with him every step of the way and had been there when he passed. She had prayed for him and with him.

Every time he wanted to give up, she told him he wasn't alone, and God knew what he went through.

Joelle made him smile when the pain was unbearable, and she had strengthened her grandmother.

His dear wife was still alive, living in a nursing home because she couldn't do anything by herself anymore. She would die soon and he was eager to be with her again.

"I'm not feeling sorry for myself. I know I shouldn't be here. This is a mistake." Joelle glared at the girl in front of her.

"Jo, you are feeling sorry for yourself. Whether you like it or not, your time is up and you are here now. If you are waiting to die again, this is a bad place for it. You can't die once you've died. The faster you get used to it, the quicker we can put you to work!"

Joelle was speechless for a moment. As upset as she had been about the harsh tone of the other angel, her attitude changed and her old enthusiasm and sassiness came back.

"Put me to work? I thought we were supposed to take it easy once we're dead. Haven't you ever heard the saying 'rest in peace'?" Her eyes sparkled, causing the other angel to smile.

"Well there's not much resting here my dear, but we have peace. I'm Taylor by the way." They shook each other's hands.

***

Taylor was a fun, energetic, straight-forward angel. Peter himself had assigned Taylor to take care of Joelle. He was the head apostle, and in charge of the guardian angels.

James, John and the other apostles took care of other things.

Right before Joelle was supposed to die, Peter had called Taylor into his office to give her the instructions she needed.

"She's really stubborn, Taylor. I know you rarely spend much time with the new angels, besides taking them to their trainer, but Joelle has great potential. We need her to start work right away. You have the right attitude and directness a woman like Joelle needs."

"Are you saying she will put up a fight about dying?"

Taylor looked at the apostle with a raised eyebrow.

"Yes! She is not expecting to die, and it will be a huge shock for her. In her mind she isn't supposed to die until she has reached a good age. It won't be easy for her to let go of her earth life. She loves it too much."

Taylor nodded. "I figured that would be the case. I've been watching her for the past few days, and she seems like someone who can be difficult, but who gives 150% when committed."

"Exactly." Peter nodded and left Taylor to it, knowing she could handle it.

***

"So now that I have your attention, Jo, shall we explore this place?"

Joelle was impressed by her surroundings and couldn't understand why she didn't notice the beauty until now. There was something calming about Taylor.

She felt she could relax, and that everything would be okay. She knew she didn't have to worry about her family anymore. They would be fine somehow, and someone would take care of them.

She looked around amazed. Everything was so beautiful, it took her breath away. Heaven sparkled like diamonds and crystal, the lakes and nature were gorgeous, and everything was so peaceful. It was like being back on earth, just this time it was perfect.

Everyone was kind, gentle, loving and honest. People hugged her and talked to her as if they had been old friends. She didn't remember them, but felt their love and friendship towards her.

"Taylor this is amazing. Why would anyone want to leave this place? Why didn't I see this before?"

"Your mind was so occupied with your death, and how you thought it was a mistake, that your eyes couldn't see past it. When we die, we don't change who we are. If we're holding onto something that might be a burden, a grudge, hate or whatever, we can't see until we are ready to let go and move on. Sometimes we need someone who is direct and straight forward to give us a little nudge."

Taylor winked at Joelle and Joelle smiled. She knew what Taylor meant.

"Wow, that's true. Thanks for the nudge, I needed it." She looked around, feeling happiness and joy again. This place was perfect. This was where she wanted to be.

Joelle had to admit that her new brown-haired friend was what she needed right now. Taylor had big brown eyes too, and her brown locks framed her face in a way that she truly looked like an angel. At five foot five, Joelle was an inch shorter than Taylor. Having her blonde hair in a cute ponytail gave her more of a sassy look.

***

"Are you ready to meet your Maker?" The question came so suddenly it startled Joelle. She didn't know what to say.

"My Maker? You mean God, our heavenly father?" she asked.

"Yes, God. Everyone sees Him after they die." Taylor smiled.

"But how can I face God? I haven't been perfect or even kind to everyone." Joelle looked worried and yet deep inside she wanted to see Him.

"He loves you, Joelle. He has waited a long time for this moment and He knows none of us are perfect, but that doesn't stop Him from loving us. That's why Jesus Christ died for us. God realizes we have many imperfections, but as long as we follow Him and do our best, He does His part too." Again Taylor smiled.

Joelle still hesitated, but then nodded in approval.

Taylor led Joelle to a large doorway. As the door swung open, bright light poured out of the building and Taylor gently pushed Joelle forward.

Jo was nervous now, but tears came to her eyes when she saw Him and felt His loving embrace. He didn't criticize, He didn't judge her. He held her in His strong arms, letting her know He loved her and that He always loved her. Soon came the goodbye, too soon. She had to leave, but there was work for her to do. It was time to accept her new reality and face a new challenge.

***

"So what happens now?" Joelle asked not knowing what to expect.

Taylor watched Joelle, wondering how she would react to what came next.

"You will receive assignments. We know your potential and want to put you right to work to take advantage of it."

Joelle didn't understand. "What assignments?" Her blue eyes were distracted, still trying to take in everything. It was busier here than on earth.

"Your first assignment will be to go back to earth. You will be a guardian angel."

"What?"

"You will live on earth, carrying out assignments to protect people and make the lives of individuals better."

"That sounds cool," Joelle said, barely hiding her excitement. Taylor smiled.

"Yes, it is cool."

"Does that mean I get superpowers and can stop evil people from hurting others?"

"Well, yes and no. You get to help make earth a better place, but you have to learn to control your powers. We can't interfere when someone does evil. After all, everyone has their free will."

Joelle looked a bit disappointed. "But some people need their butts kicked."

Again Taylor smiled about Joelle's passion and enthusiasm. Joelle would do well.

"Yes Jo, you'll get to kick butts, putting it in your words. That being said, you must do it with kindness and love, no matter how much you want to protect those who are being treated unfairly."

Joelle bit her lip. She always did that when she was thinking.

"I will bring you to earth and put you into the care of your trainer. He's the perfect match for you and has the patience he needs to train you."

Taylor smirked when she saw Joelle's shocked look.

"What's that supposed to mean? The perfect match? Talk about match-made-in-heaven, huh? And he has the patience he needs to train me? Are you trying to say I'm difficult?"

Taylor laughed out loud. She loved Joelle's sarcastic and dry sense of humor and would miss her when she left for the assignment, but all in good time. It wouldn't be goodbye forever.

"How do we get to earth? And why do you have to take me? Just tell me how to do it."

Taylor chuckled. Joelle had such a determined look on her face.

"To be honest, I'm afraid if I let you go alone you might wander off and take over the world – dealing justice to the bad guys."

Now Joelle laughed. "You've got a point there. That sounds like something I'd do."

She winked at Taylor and both of them chuckled.

"So what superpowers do I have now?" Joelle's curiosity took over.

"I knew you'd ask," Taylor responded.

"Well, I'm just bracing myself to conquer the world."

Taylor smiled again.

"You will be able to stop time, calm people down, and have superhuman strength."

"That is awesome. I will arm wrestle the strongest dudes on earth and when I'm done with them, they won't know what hit them."

"You're so funny, Jo. You'll have everyone beat just with your personality and by using your remarkable sense of humor."

Taylor couldn't stop laughing. Just the thought of Joelle standing up to a six-foot eight inch guy and challenging him to an arm wrestling match made her laugh out loud.

Joelle wore a big grin on her face. She was back to her normal self.

They reached the big entrance again, and it was time for Joelle to say goodbye to heaven and go back to earth.

She hugged her grandfather, and everyone else that came for her little farewell, then Taylor snapped her fingers and with a big poof she and Joelle were gone. A moment later, they stepped out of a closet.

2.   Guardian Angel Agency

"Why am I dressed differently now? What happened to my white dress and where did these clothes come from?"

Joelle was more than confused. Her white dress had disappeared and instead she wore a knee-length dark blue skirt with a white blouse and comfortable business shoes.

Taylor grinned. "We only wear the white dresses in heaven. When you're on earth, you can wear whatever you want. It has to be modest and suitable though."

"But how did I get these clothes?"

"It happens automatically."

"Does that mean I'll always wear the same clothes?" Joelle asked still looking confused.

"No, you can change your clothes to anything you want. Just think about whatever attire you'd like, and your clothing will change right away."

Joelle pictured wearing her favorite running shoes and a dark blue coat, and sure enough a moment later her clothes had changed.

"Cool!" Jo grinned from ear to ear and returned her clothes to the dark blue skirt and white blouse, but kept her running shoes - just because.

Then she noticed the room Taylor had taken them to.

"Where are we?" Joelle looked around. It looked like a comfortable, beautifully arranged office. There were dark desks in the room, nice looking leather couches and seats, plants, big windows and beautiful blue curtains.

"We're at the GAA in Edinburgh, Scotland."

"Holy cow! I will live in Scotland now? Do you know how hard it is to understand the people here?"

"Yes I do, but as an angel you can understand any language or accent without a problem." Taylor grinned as she saw how happy and excited Joelle was. The ability to understand other languages was music to Joelle's ears. "Plus you should feel right at home with your dry sense of humor."

Another big smile lit Taylor's face.

"So what's with the angels I saw in heaven? Are they taking a break up there, or do only some of us work?"

Taylor saw the sassy sparkle in Joelle's eyes and grinned.

"Everyone has their own job. There's plenty to do in heaven. I, for example, am a coordinator. I coordinate where everyone goes, what jobs need to be filled, and which angels stay in heaven or go to earth."

"But our assignments and jobs change, right? Or do we do the same job for the rest of forever?"

"We get moved around to wherever we are needed at the time, since we have different talents and strengths. That way we don't get bored." She winked at Joelle.

"What's my grandfather's job right now? Plus, I never saw my other grandparents. Where are they?"

"Your grandfather is a pre-mortality instructor."

"A what?"

"A pre-mortality instructor. He teaches those who have yet to be born and prepares them for their journey. The pre-mortality teaching team teaches about the premortal existence, agency and what to expect during earth life. They also assist the post-mortality team in teaching those who came back and haven't heard of God, or weren't as good as they should have been, about repentance, the Atonement, resurrection and exaltation.

We don't change who we are when we die. We still have our free will and can choose if we want to follow God or the devil. Peter gives all our instructors a special teaching priesthood blessing so they have the right to teach the gospel of Jesus Christ.

Your deceased paternal grandparents are in Chile right now. They're assigned to a hospital."

"Do guardian angels have to be from a certain church, to be guardian angels?"

Taylor looked at her puzzled.

"What I mean is, I am a member of the Church of Jesus Christ of Latter-day Saints. Are all guardian angels LDS?"

"A lot of the guardian angels are LDS, but you don't need to be a member of the LDS church to protect humans from harm. To earn the right to be a guardian angel you have to be a good human and try your best in following our Savior. We have many wonderful guardian angels from different religions.

Things made more sense to Joelle, and yet she still had lots of questions. Everything was overwhelming, and there was much to learn.

"What is the GAA?" Joelle asked looking puzzled as she remembered that Taylor had mentioned it earlier.

"GAA stands for Guardian Angel Agency. These are our headquarters - here in Edinburgh at least. You will make new friends quickly. The angel apartments, called flats here in Britain, are above this building, but humans can't see them. They only see this office building."

"Wow, so does that mean this building belongs to the GAA, or do humans use these offices as well? I mean this office looks modern with the furniture and technology in here."

"No, humans never come in here. This building is only used by us angels."

"But doesn't that confuse humans? If I walked by this building every single day for years, and saw an empty office, I would start to wonder."

"To the humans this place isn't an office, but a house in which people live. To keep the illusion, we even have one or two of us leave the building every so often looking like normal humans and not angels."

"Cool. Does that mean I can make myself visible?"

"Yes you can, but you shouldn't use said ability against humans, not even to scare the life out of evil people."

A big huge smile appeared on Joelle's face.

"Darn it! That would be fun. I bet if I did that a few times, they wouldn't dare hurt anyone anymore."

"Jo!"

"Yes, yes, I get it, and I will try to behave."

***

A swooshing sound was heard and a tall, young man appeared in the room. Taylor greeted him with a hug, obviously happy to see him. Joelle had time to study him while he was engaged in conversation with Taylor. He had dark blonde hair and wore dark coloured trousers with a white shirt.

Hmm, not bad looking for an angel. Handsome guy, she thought.

Taylor laughed out loud and the young man turned around looking at her with a huge grin.

"Thank you, Joelle."

She blushed and wanted to hide in a hole. Had she said that out loud? No, she was sure she hadn't.

The young man winked at her and her face turned to a darker shade of red.

"Taylor, look at that, a blushing angel, how cute."

Joelle rolled her eyes, and Taylor laughed even harder.

"Awesome, does that mean, you guys can read my mind?"

Taylor nodded. "Yes we can. Sorry, I forgot to mention it."

"Yeah, right you're sorry. You're enjoying this way too much."

Taylor chuckled.

"So how come I can't read your minds? It would have been nice to get a warning that I shouldn't be thinking certain things."

Her sarcasm made the young man smile.

"You will be able to read minds too, Joelle, all in good time," he said and Taylor added: "And we can only read minds when we're next to someone. If we're somewhere far off, we can't hear what you're thinking, and you have your privacy back. Plus, you will learn to control your thoughts, which will make it hard for anyone to read your mind."

"Nice. I've got at least that to look forward to. So, no more thinking for me." She winked at them both and made it clear that she wasn't angry, and hadn't taken offence to them not telling her they could read her mind.

"Do I at least get to read the humans' minds?"

"Yes you do. And may I introduce you to your trainer? This is Josh."

He bowed like a gentleman trying to make her blush again, but this time she was ready for it. She gave him a sassy grin and dropped a curtsy.

Taylor burst out laughing and Josh joined in.

"Okay, it's time for me to leave. Josh will take over now, and you will meet your roommates later."

She gave Joelle a big hug, wishing her the best.

"Don't forget that you just need to be yourself. Now get out there and show everyone that God loves them and that He is always there for them. Nobody is forgotten."

It was hard for her to leave Joelle. For the first time in her ten years of being an angel she wanted to keep this new friend with her in heaven and not share her with the world. Josh smiled understandingly at Taylor, gave her a hug, and she was gone.

***

Joelle felt uneasy and sad. Taylor had been kind, almost like family. It was strange, but in just the short time she knew Taylor, she felt they had known each other forever and were best friends. Their personalities were perfect for each other. Having to get used to something and someone else wouldn't be easy.

Not wanting Josh to know how she felt, she turned to him.

"So what's my first assignment?"

In a brotherly way he put his arm around her shoulders.

"Our first assignment is a twelve-year-old girl. Her name is Hannah, and her parents died in a car accident six months ago. She has been in foster care, in and out of several orphanages, and keeps escaping. She is very stubborn and we think you can help."

Joelle gave him a sly look.

"What is it with you angels and my stubbornness? You always have to rub it in, huh?"

He smiled. "Being stubborn isn't always a bad thing. Here it's good because we're hoping that you're more stubborn than she is."

"So what do you want me to do? Catch her and tie her to a bed in the orphanage?"

Again he smiled. "No of course not! We want you to make friends with her and find her a new home she will love and accept."

"Okay, that sounds fair. So what do you do while I'm working?"

He gave her a nudge. "Cheeky girl. I'm here to teach you how to behave and not use your special powers."

"Good luck with that!"

"That's what I'm telling myself too."

She elbowed him in his stomach.

"Ouch, be careful, young lady." He narrowed his eyes to a slit, trying to look intimidating, but she only laughed at him.

"You started it, so stop being such a wimp."

That left him speechless for a moment. He glared at her and then grinned from ear to ear.

"How can such a small person be so quick-witted?" He nudged her again, putting his arm around her shoulders. "Don't forget I'm six foot three and can take you any time."

Now it was her turn to narrow her eyes and flash him a sideways glance.

"Don't you dare use your height against me!" She gave him a smile.

"What are you going to teach me first, Mister Tall?"

He noticed the mocking tone in her voice and held back a clever remark. He liked her already and knew he would get along with her.

"First, I need to show you how to use your new powers. But don't forget to only use them when suitable. You're not allowed to interfere with someone's choices."

She looked at him with a cheeky expression, but nodded.

"If you want to stop time, touch the tips of your forefingers together quickly. To start time again, tap them together the same way, but don't overuse this power since it messes up everyone else's time as well."

"Can any of the other angels undo my time-stopping?"

"No they can't, and that's why you have to be careful when you do it."

"Okay."

"If you want to calm people down, all you need to do is stare in their eyes. They will calm down at once."

She nodded her head in approval.

"Will it still work if I'm invisible?"

"Yes it will."

She smiled. "Awesome."

"If you want to make yourself visible, just wiggle your nose or pull your ear."

"Yeah right!" Joelle wasn't sure if he was mocking her, or if this was how it worked, so she decided not to believe him at this point.

"No really, that's how you do it."

She stared at him, not sure how to go ahead, but then called his bluff.

"Okay, go on then, show me how it's done." She was determined not to look like a fool, but Josh only shook his head.

"I'm just explaining everything right now so you must trust me." Still not convinced, she let it go for now.

"Do all guardian angels have the same powers?" Joelle asked.

"Yes and no. We all have the ability to stop time, calm down humans and angels, use our super strength, and read minds. But there are angels out there who have special powers on top of the normal powers."

"How do we know if we have a special power? Do they tell you in heaven before taking you to your trainer?"

"Mostly yes. Or the angels learn about them later on when they're ready. Also, some special powers come with assignments."

"Does every angel know about the special powers out there?"

"Not always. There are powers that are rare, and not talked about, that only Peter knows about. He tells no one except those who have the powers since he doesn't want angels to mess with them and use the powers for bad things."

"Do you know how angels get special powers and why only certain angels have them?"

"Not exactly, no. I'm guessing those angels earn them in their human life."

Joelle nodded. She realised that Josh didn't know much about it. She probably would find out more as time went on. Maybe at one point she would even meet an angel with special powers.

"So what about our superhuman strength? You said nothing about it while I've asked you these questions." She winked at him and he grinned.

"You don't have to do anything for your strength. It will be with you at all times."

"Does that mean I'm stronger than you?" There was that same cheeky smile on her face from before.

"Want to try?" Before she could even reply he put his hands on her hips and lifted her in the air. She tried to break free, but no matter how much she tried to loosen his grip, she was stuck there in the air.

"Hey let me down. Sure you can pick me up like a leaf now. I'm an angel and probably weigh nothing."

"Wrong. An angel lifting another angel is like a human lifting another human, except we have a lot more strength."

"Okay fine, would you please let me down now? You've showed off your manly angel strength long enough."

She had blushed again and wanted to get away from him. He had noticed her blushing and put her down with a grin.

"Do male and female angels have equal strength, or is there a difference?"

"It's the same as when you were human. Men are usually stronger than women."

"But with my strength, I can kick human guys' butts, right?"

He looked at her with a raised eyebrow.

"Sure, but don't forget that I can read your mind, and will stop you from doing anything that will abuse your powers."

"Does that mean we're together 24/7?"

"No, at night when the humans are asleep, we return to our flats to get rest ourselves. As angel we don't sleep, but we rest our spiritual bodies. That's the time we get to enjoy private time and escape in memories. But don't think you can sneak away and do whatever you please when I'm not around you anymore. Your angel roommates are informed and will keep an eye on you… and so will the night shift angels."

A big smile appeared on his face. She couldn't believe her ears.

"They are informed about me? Are you trying to say I'm an uncontrollable person or something?"

"No, but we've heard you're hard-headed and might do something of which the rest of us don't approve."

She sighed dramatically, rolled her eyes and sat down.

"Hey, I can follow rules, but I'm not too happy about these restrictions on my freedom!"

He laughed at her sarcasm. "You'll be just fine. Behave yourself and we'll give you your freedom."

"Oh that's so kind of you."

"I know, that's how I am." He winked at her and made her smile too.

"What do you mean with angel roommates?" She asked confused.

"Well, there are many angels in this agency, and we share flats and rooms with them. It's like having roommates as a human." He grinned at her again and then snapped his fingers. A second later both stood outside the building.

***

The house was typical Scottish architecture. It had a ground and first floor, had brown-greyish bricks, large windows, and a red wooden door with the traditional old metal door knocker. It reminded Joelle of the Jane Austen movies she had watched. Now she understood why humans didn't think of this as an office building, but a home. The outside had a homely touch, and the curtains were mostly closed so people couldn't look inside.

She was gradually understanding everything more, and all this began to make sense to her.

The surrounding buildings were old and had an antique touch to it. Right above the agency, she noticed the flats added on for the angels. It was the same style, and yet more elegant with a special sparkle to it. She knew that none of the humans could see the added levels.

"Are we invisible, or can they see us?" Her eyes were still glued to the beautiful old building behind them.

"They can't see us right now. I want to show you around and get you familiar with the city before you're seen. Also, I will be invisible most of the time we are working. So remember that, when visible and you talk to me in public, because you'll look like a mad person talking to yourself."

She rolled her eyes again. "Thank you for pointing out the obvious. I never would have guessed that, especially after you mentioned you'll be invisible most of the time. DUH!"

He couldn't help but smile at her sarcasm.

"Don't mention it."

She raised her eyebrow and followed him down the street.

"So the humans can't hear, see or feel us at all when we're invisible?"

"No they can't. It's as if we don't exist. They have no idea how many guardian angels are around them."

Suddenly, as if on cue to back up his words, two black haired girls waved at them from the other side of the street.

"Oi Josh, the new lass?"

"Yes, that's right."

"Brilliant. Cheerio!" And they were gone.

"I'm assuming that since they saw us they were guardian angels too?"

"Such a clever girl you are."

She turned her head, trying to find more.

They reached Princess Street and walked along a busy road. A few drunk teenagers pushed each other.

Joelle watched them ready to jump in if things got out of hand. And sure enough, one of them pushed his friend too hard, and he stepped off the pavement and fell on the street right in front of a huge lorry.

Before Joelle could react, Josh grabbed her arm and held her back.

"We have to help…" she said, but just then, two male angels stepped in, stopping the lorry just in time.

Several people had watched the whole scene, frightfully expecting the crash, as the lorry driver tried to stop his vehicle. Nobody thought he'd be able to stop.

Joelle had held her breath too, not knowing what to expect. Relieved, she relaxed.

"So how come those guys got to help? I thought we're not allowed to interfere."

"You wanted to jump in yourself!" he said reminding her of the fact that he had to hold her back.

"Yes, well that was a reflex."

He grinned at her. "You're an interesting person, Joelle. For your information, we can and should help when something gets out of control, like when someone will be injured or killed in an accident. Those drunk blokes were being stupid and didn't realise how dangerous their behaviour was. That's when their guardian angels stepped in and stopped things from happening. Sometimes we at least make it so it isn't as bad as it could be unless it's time for them to die."

"Oh I see, but we're not allowed to get involved when someone purposely tries to hurt or kill someone? Like if those blokes wouldn't have been drunk, but had pushed him into the street to harm or kill him on purpose?"

Joelle looked confused when she realised that she had used the British word for 'guys' without even thinking about it. Apparently the different words used in the country, entered her vocabulary after hearing them.

"Correct, and as long as a guardian angel is around his human, he should be the one jumping in to protect his human before any other guardian angel gets involved. That's why I stopped you earlier."

"Are there times when a guardian angel is not around their human?"

"Yes, when they get attacked by evil angels," he explained.

"The evil angels are here, around us?" She asked looking around worried. She had always been afraid of evil spirits as a human. The thought of them being close by right now was not pleasant.

"Oh yes, they make our jobs miserable and try to make us fail all the time."

"How do I recognise if an angel is good or evil?"

"You will be able to tell straight away, trust me."

Walking down Princess Street, she noticed several guardian angels, always on the look-out. They stepped in when someone slipped and fell. Every time someone needed help, they were there. It made her realise that humans are much more protected than they could ever imagine.

"Tell me, Josh. Are these angels everywhere?"

"Yes they are."

"So when I was alive and rescued that baby, why wasn't I protected?"

He noticed the accusing tone in her voice.

"Your time was up, Jo. Your angels knew your human life was over. That's why they stepped back and did nothing."

"Oh," Joelle thought about that for a moment. "That must be hard for a guardian angel to not do anything, when they've protected someone for so long?"

"You have no idea. It is devastating not to get involved, but better things are in store for them and we'll see them again soon. That's when we can tell them we used to be their guardian angel."

He smiled at her, knowing how she felt right now. Several thoughts ran through her head that made her sad and yet excited for the future.

"Yes Jo, you'll be able to talk to your guardian angels too at one point. There are always lots of angels around, but they're in pairs assigned to one person. Right now your last two are still in the States, but sometime in the future you'll be able to meet them."

He noticed the puzzled look on her face and her confused thoughts.

She looked up to him, and this time her eyes didn't look cheeky or sarcastic, just grateful and sweet. He couldn't help but put his arm around her shoulders and smile back at her.

Once they reached Edinburgh Castle, they watched the sunset, and Joelle was impressed with the beautiful panoramic view of the city. She felt right at home here and knew this was the right place for her, right now.

"In a few months, they will have the Edinburgh Military Tattoo here. You'll love that. It's one time when we work our hardest to protect the humans, but well worth it."

Hearing that got her excited. She had heard about the tattoo before and was looking forward to it.

They walked back along High Street and Josh showed her Holyrood Park, the biggest park in central Edinburgh. She loved it.

Since it was now getting dark and late, they walked back to the office.

"So now it's the night shift angels that take over protecting the humans? We can't leave the humans to themselves during the night, correct?"

"That's right, we can't. We work in shifts, but can jump in and take action at once when something big happens. Each of us has a built-in alarm system that lets us know. Like when there is a train accident. Everyone working in the area responds at once to keep the damage to a minimum."

That made sense. She had always wondered about that.

"And when 9/11 happened?"

"The same thing. Every guardian angel around went there to help. We even had angels that work in heaven come down to give us a hand. If we had not worked our bums off, along with those hard working humans, things would have been much worse. Those who didn't make it to work on time, or weren't in the buildings during the attacks, was angels' doing."

"Man, too bad we can't tell that to the humans who keep complaining and attacking God for not keeping it from happening."

"Yes they do not understand what they're talking about. Heavenly Father doesn't want things like that to happen, but when the evil angels take charge and influence humans so badly that they won't listen to us anymore, He can only do so much. He wants us to have our free will, and that includes everyone, even the bad blokes. He doesn't take it away just because the evil angels influence humans to do bad things. If He did that, we wouldn't have much freedom to choose, now would we? We choose whether we want to be good or evil. He respects that even though it's hard for Him and makes Him sad when His children hate and hurt each other."

Joelle was impressed. She remembered, from her human life, how important agency was to Heavenly Father. That was something they had discussed in church many times.

"So how can we change that some humans blame God when bad things happen?"

"We can't. Every human would have to accept that evil angels exist, that they have their freedom to choose, and that they should not judge God too quickly. The evil angels don't want that to happen. They want mankind to be miserable. Plus, not everyone believes in God and we have to tolerate and accept that just as much as we want others to accept and tolerate that we believe in God."

Joelle realised at that moment what a wise person Josh was. She knew she could learn so much from him.

"Will I meet Hannah today?"

"No, not today. She still has her other two guardian angels around, but they will leave tomorrow."

"Why don't they get to stay with her and finish the assignment?"

"Not every guardian angel has special assignments. Sometimes we're just out there to protect a human. We also only get a certain amount of time to do an assignment. If angels don't succeed, it means the human isn't ready or willing to work with them, or it wasn't the right time for the assignment to be finished."

"Does that mean they failed?"

"No it means they tried their best, but will do better at a different job, or it wasn't the right time. We are still the same people we were before we died. Which means if someone is impatient, they will still be impatient as an angel. If someone dies who was kind and stubborn, they

41

will be the same after death. Now that you and I are assigned to Hannah, we have to do our best to make it work. It doesn't mean that we are better than the other angels, but it means we are better suited right now and Hannah is more prepared.

It was late once they reached the office building.

Joelle noticed that a huge group of guardian angels were leaving while others returned home. It was shift change.

Josh took her upstairs and led her to her flat.

"That sure was an interesting day, Jo. I don't think I will ever be bored with you."

She winked at him. "I hope that's a good thing!"

He laughed, gave her a hug and off he went.

***

When she opened the door, she realised how huge the flat was. It had ten bedrooms with two beds each. Four girls greeted her happily.

"Hi Joelle, nice to meet you. I've heard a lot of good things about you," said a tall girl with black hair as she stepped closer. "My name is Jade."

She looked like someone who'd be easy to get along. She was outgoing and friendly.

Now two redheads greeted her. "Hi, I'm Sydney. I'll be your roommate," she said as she smiled at Joelle.

Jo liked her right away. Sydney seemed more of a quiet but kind person, and Joelle looked forward to getting to know her more.

The other redhead was also tall, but serious. She shook Joelle's hand and told her that her name was Crystal.

Marissa was the last one that greeted Joelle. She was shy and quiet and left the room straight away after greeting her, followed by Crystal and Jade.

"Are you hungry, Jo?" Sydney asked, not waiting to call Joelle by her nickname. Joelle liked that.

"I am not sure, do we eat as angels?" she asked not knowing if she was hungry or not. Everything had been so crazy and overwhelming all day long she hadn't even thought about food.

"Oh sure we eat. That's one of the best inventions ever," Sydney said as she gave her odd looking food that tasted fantastic.

"What's this?"

"Fruits and vegetables from heaven. Even though we don't have human bodies anymore, we still have to keep our spiritual body strong, and this stuff is brilliant."

"It sure is, I don't think I have ever eaten anything so delicious."

Sydney smiled.

"So how many guardian angels live here?" Joelle asked looking around.

"Oh, thousands of angels. This is just one of many flats. We're divided into teams, so you'll most likely only get to know a small group of angels. The rest you'll see now and then, but you won't work with them. Josh is our team leader at the moment. When something big comes up everyone in our team goes to him, but we have plenty of teams and angels around us."

Joelle was impressed. This was a well-organised agency.

After she finished eating, Joelle remembered something else she wanted to ask.

"Tell me, Sydney, when we want to make ourselves visible, do we really pull our ear or wiggle our nose?"

Sydney laughed. "That's so Josh. It's the little prank he pulls on the new angels to see if they'll try."

"I knew it," Joelle said with a cheeky smile on her face, "that stinker!"

Sydney sat down, still smiling.

"So how do we make ourselves visible or invisible?" Joelle asked looking at her roommate.

"You fold your arms and blink with both eyes."

"Nu uh!" Joelle knew for sure this time, that this was another joke. Sydney laughed.

"No, I'm teasing you. All you have to do is snap your middle finger and thumb of your right hand. The same movement with your left hand can move you wherever you want to go, once you are fully trained."

That sounded better and Joelle tried it right away.

"Cool!" she said once she was gone.

Sydney smiled again. She liked Joelle a great deal and hoped that she could work with her eventually. For now, she was a trainer herself, just like Josh.

Sydney's trainee Paul was a difficult angel. He was a proud fellow and tried to do everything by himself. He took off alone, tried to impress human and angel girls, but he had a great gift in dealing with little children.

Sydney was his third trainer already, and he had only been in training for three weeks. She was easy going, and laid back, which helped. He went through two trainers during the first week, and she had been with him for a fortnight. Her kind, straightforward and forgiving nature was a good match for him. He was tall, not bad looking, but arrogant.

Sydney couldn't help but wonder how Joelle would react when she met Paul for the first time.

That's what the other angels were thinking too. The angels on night shift couldn't help but feel sorry for themselves since they would miss it. Everyone resting right now couldn't wait for the next day to start.

Paul himself looked forward to meeting the new girl. He knew he was good looking and convinced the new angel would fall in love with him.

He wanted to know every single detail about her. Since he was Josh's roommate, he kept talking Josh's ear off.

Josh was an easy going, patient person, but Paul was a challenge for him because he was so self-centred. Josh had to keep reminding himself that Paul had good qualities and that he shouldn't think ill of anyone.

He felt sorry for Joelle because Paul would look at her as his new toy, until another new female angel joined the group. At the same time Josh was curious how Joelle would react to Paul. Joelle was stubborn and outspoken. She wouldn't just stand still and let things happen if she felt it wasn't right.

While Paul talked, Josh lost himself in memories of his earth life. That was the only way he could escape his less-than-pleasant roommate and relax.

***

Seven am the next morning was shift change. Jade and Crystal, Marissa and a girl Joelle hadn't seen the night before, stepped out of their room. The girl Joelle hadn't met yet, had a curvy figure and was friendly and always smiling. Since Marissa was so shy it seemed to be a good match. The girl's name was Destinee, and she had come from Australia a few months before, so her accent was still pretty thick.

They snapped their fingers and appeared in the office. The room was packed with angels. Joelle had to search the room before she found her trainer.

Josh was happy to be rid of Paul and he greeted Joelle with a big smile. But before Josh could give her a hug, Paul had pushed himself between them and hugged Joelle instead.

Joelle was shocked that a man hugged her with no warning. He hadn't even introduced himself to her and so she shoved Paul to the side while glancing at her trainer. Josh shook his head annoyed.

Everyone else watched to see what would happen.

"Hi Sweetie. I'm Paul. I know Josh is your trainer, but if you have questions you can always come to me."

He looked deep into her blue eyes and she stepped back.

So far she had not felt uncomfortable around anyone, but this person stepped too close for her liking. Besides that, she was surprised that an angel flirted this way. Not to mention that he had hugged her without even knowing her.

"Hi Paul, I'm Joelle." Her voice sounded annoyed and distant, but Paul didn't seem to notice that.

He shook her hand with a big grin on his face, holding it longer than necessary.

"You're gorgeous, sweetheart and we will be great friends. Maybe once our year of training is over we can be partners, but we should get together for a date soon."

He winked at her, still smiling, still holding her hand. Jo took her hand from him and stepped backwards.

She politely smiled and tried to walk past him, but he stepped in her way again. It was getting harder and harder for her to bite her tongue, but he had no right to invade her personal space that way. He made too many passes at her.

"No offence, but no thank you."

"Don't be shy, sweetheart. Just admit I'm handsome and stunning."

"Excuse me?"

"I know you want to be with me. You and I have much in common. We're both new, we're both single and we're meant for each other. After all there has to be a reason why we're both here. We were destined to meet."

"How do you know I am single, Paul? Besides, I'm here because a girl named Hannah needs me and nothing else."

"Someone as gorgeous as you is not here for a simple assignment. Babe, your beauty makes the morning sun look like the dull glimmer of the moon.[2]"

Josh almost gagged when he heard the chat-up line.

Joelle herself wasn't sure whether she should gag or explode. He wasn't getting it that she wasn't interested, and had totally ignored her remark about her relationship status. She was not someone that let anyone sweet-talk her.

"Okay that's enough for now. I'm done here." She tried to step away, but once again Paul was in her way, giving her a winning smile.

"Would you grab my arm so I can tell my friends I've been touched by an angel?[3]" He tried to make a joke, but it was bad timing. Joelle was ticked off now. Before she could respond, he continued: "For a moment I thought I

[2]/3 Christian pick-up lines, Internet, 2013

48

had died again and gone to heaven. Now I see I'm very much alive, and that instead heaven has been brought to me.[4]" He grinned from ear to ear while everyone else in the room shook their head. Everyone except Joelle.

"Okay, that does it. Listen pretty boy, you're self-centred and weird. I'm not interested in your cheesy and corn-flavoured chat-up lines, and I'm not interested in a relationship. So please stop flirting with me. And stop calling me sweetheart or sweetie, my name is Joelle!"

"Why are you getting so upset, sweetie? Is it because you like what I'm saying? So when do you want to go on a date?"

He still had a wide smile on his face which made Joelle's temper boil even more. Before things escalated, and as Joelle was about to snap, Josh grabbed Joelle's arm and pulled her away from Paul.

Everyone else in the room had to hide a smile, but luckily it was time to get to work.

Before Paul stepped closer to Joelle again, Sydney snapped her fingers and she and Paul were gone.

As soon as Joelle saw Paul and Sydney disappear, and the other angels had left, she exploded.

"Stone the crows, what in the world was that? Did you know he was like that?"

"Yes, but…" before he could continue she interrupted.

---

[4] Christian pick-up line, Internet, 2013

"Why didn't you warn me about him? That bloke is mad! How can he be a guardian angel if he flirts with girls like that? He should be locked up in a place somewhere, banished from women."

She took a deep breath and Josh had to smile.

"What's so funny? That was not cool. I mean did you hear his slimy chat-up lines? How can so much rubbish come out of someone's mouth? His flirting was so corny and cheesy that I expected a bag of cheddar popcorn to shoot out of his mouth. I mean it's one thing if someone tactfully tries to see if the other person is interested, but this bloke is a flirting machine and didn't listen to a thing I said. How can anyone assume the other person is interested? And then this stepping in my way and coming close to me…. the nerve he had to hug me without even knowing me. If he tries to do that again I will beat him up."

Joelle looked furious, but seeing her go off amused Josh.

"I bet you would," he said.

"I totally will."

He gave her a cheeky smile, and it made her smile too.

"Seriously Josh, that's not normal behaviour. Why is he here?"

"He's fantastic with children."

"And?"

"That's why he's here."

"Whoa, I have to avoid that freak or else I will explode."

"You will explode? What was this just now?"

"That was me letting off steam in a loud way."

Josh laughed out loud. Good thing she had her humour back.

"Has he ever tried to hit on Sydney?"

"Right from the beginning, but I've never seen him ask her on a date."

She blushed.

"Okay, okay I get it. Nice, like that makes me feel better!"

With a big grin he put his arm around her and snapped his fingers.

3. Meeting Hannah

"Josh, they caught Hannah again and took her to the orphanage," two female angels said as they appeared.

"Okay, thanks for letting us know. Jo, these are Faith and Blossom. They've been watching over Hannah and are being transferred to Seattle and Beijing."

"Cool, nice to meet you."

"Nice to meet you too, Jo. Good luck with Hannah. She's a good lass, but stubborn. Cheerio," Faith said, and they were gone again.

"That was a quick visit."

"Yes, they are angel-workaholics and keep busy. They never stay longer than just a few seconds. So Hannah is in the orphanage now. I want you to meet her right away. Do you want to be my wife?" he asked with a big grin on his face as he looked at her. It made her speechless and once again she blushed.

"Excuse me?"

"Well, we need to act like a married couple to make them believe we're interested in adopting."

"Oh phew! Geez Josh! Stop teasing me, I almost had a heart attack."

"No matter, a heart attack won't do much since you're already dead. Besides, you said you find me attractive."

"JOSH! Stop that!"

Her face looked like a tomato, and his big grin didn't help the situation. She elbowed him in the stomach and that made him laugh even more.

"Okay, okay, Jo. Please stop beating me up!"

"I haven't even started yet, so you'd better watch out. Besides, I never SAID anything, you rudely listened to my thoughts. And as far as I remember, the word in my THOUGHTS was not 'attractive'!"

"Oh I am sorry, my mistake. You are right, you found me 'handsome', not attractive!" He smirked wide when she continued to blush.

"I seriously don't believe this, Josh! Are all trainers so rude and cheeky? If not, I am demanding a new trainer!" He laughed out loud.

Pretending to be angry at him, she kept on walking. A moment later, he knelt before her begging forgiveness.

Now she laughed out loud too. "JOSH! You're such a tease!"

"I know, but it's so fun to tease you. It's the way you react to it, so cute and charming."

He jumped back on his feet. "So, are you ready to meet Hannah?"

"Yes. I can't wait to meet her."

***

The orphanage was a large, grey building. It didn't look inviting, but when they went inside, it was playful, colourful and welcoming. Joelle's feeling told her that this was a good place.

Josh gave her a sign that they needed to make themselves visible now. He waited for her to wiggle her nose or pull her ear, but she didn't.

"Blimey, who told you?"

She grinned at him. "Sydney, since she is nice." She raised an eyebrow.

"But how did that come up?" he asked, surprised.

"I asked her about it. I didn't trust your explanation and wanted to make sure."

"Wow, you're a clever little thing aren't you?" Josh asked impressed. Normally, new trainees were so overwhelmed with everything, that they didn't pay attention to little things like how to make yourself visible. He thought he had fooled her. Apparently not.

"Yes, I can tell when someone is trying to tease me." She winked at him and he laughed.

Now it was time to make themselves visible, and they did. They knocked on the main office door and stepped in.

An old, but friendly woman greeted them.

"Guid morning! Can A gie ye a haund?" she said with a strong Scottish accent.

"Good morning. My name is Josh McIntosh, and this is my wife, Joelle. We're thinking of adopting a child."

"Nice tae meit ye! Whaur ar ye frae?"

"From all over the world. I was born in Dundee and my wife is from New York." Joelle looked at Josh with a surprised look.

"D'ye spaek Scots?"

Josh grinned and nodded.

The lady looked at Joelle now. "Aye, juist a wee bit."

Confused, the woman got up. "Ho ye!" She left the room through a side door.

***

"You were born in Dundee? I don't hear a Scottish accent. You sound American." Joelle raised an eyebrow and wasn't sure what to think. He grinned.

"I said I was born in Dundee not that I lived there my whole life," he said with a smile on his face.

"You were born in Scotland?" Joelle looked at him with an expression that told him she didn't believe him.

"No," he had to admit. "I said that so they wouldn't give us any grief about adopting a child."

55

"You lied? I see," Joelle said with a sarcastic grin on her face and Josh gave her nudge.

"I didn't lie, just stretched the truth a wee bit." He winked at her and grinned. "And I have Scottish ancestors."

"Sure!" She grinned too, but before he could say more, another lady entered the room. She had an elegant presence about her.

"Good morning, what can I do for you?"

"Good morning. My name is Josh McIntosh, and this is my wife Joelle. I'm assuming you're from England?"

"Yes I am young man," she said smiling. "Please have a seat."

They both sat down. "I'm Katherine Carter and run the orphanage. Are you here to adopt a child?"

"We are thinking about it, yes."

"What age are you considering?"

"We would like to adopt an older child, around twelve years old?"

"Oh yes. We only have one here now. A girl named Hannah. Let me guide you into the meeting room and then I will fetch her at once."

She took them into a smaller living room and left.

Joelle felt nervous. *What if Hannah didn't like her or wouldn't trust her?* Josh pulled her into his arms, looking right into her eyes.

"She will love you. Just give it time." She immediately felt calmer.

"That's not fair, Josh! You can even use that power on me?"

"Yes I can," he said as a big grin lit up his face.

"Does that mean we can calm down humans and angels?" Joelle asked, and he nodded.

"Angels can also be calmed down by touch, and not just by staring into their eyes."

"By touch?" Joelle looked confused.

"Yes. Instead of staring in the eyes of another guardian angel, I can put my hands on their shoulder or arm and it will calm them down too. The calming touch is not as powerful as the stare though. If the other angel is not willing to be calmed down, or might even fight it, it won't work. Staring in someone's eyes is the only thing that works always, and 100%, but the other angel has to look at you."

The door opened and Mrs. Carter came back, followed by a red headed girl.

"Mr. and Mrs. McIntosh, this is Hannah."

Jo smiled at the twelve-year-old. Hannah looked at them with a stern and angry look.

"I will leave you three for a moment."

Mrs. Carter patted Hannah's shoulder, gave her an encouraging smile and then left the room.

"I'm not interested in being adopted." Hannah pressed her lips together and sat in a chair.

Josh and Joelle also sat down. Joelle was surprised that Hannah had an English accent, too.

"Oh, we're just looking around. No worries." Joelle continued to smile at her. "This is Josh and I'm Jo. How do you like it here?"

"I don't like it here, and will not stay long."

Josh and Joelle both knew her last remark was a challenge. She was testing to see if they would tell Mrs. Carter.

"Really? Where are you going?"

"No idea, but I want to be free."

"But don't you want a mum and a dad, Hannah?"

"I need no one."

The child was cold and reserved towards them, and it was hard for Joelle to read her mind.

"Can we at least be friends?" Joelle asked.

That was a question Hannah didn't expect, and it made her speechless for a moment. Before she could respond, Mrs. Carter stepped back into the room.

"Okay that's enough for today. Hannah, you can go back upstairs." Without looking at anyone, the girl left the room.

"What do you think?" Katherine Carter looked worried. She had only given them a few minutes to make sure Hannah wouldn't scare them off right away.

"We like her. She seems like a sweet child and would fit into our little family."

Mrs. Carter seemed surprised. She had known Hannah for several months now and not only did she keep running away, but was rude, cold and reserved. She didn't make it easy for anyone to like or love her.

Hannah stood just outside the door listening to every word. She too was surprised. Couples that met her had always said nasty things about her, and never liked her. She had to admit she had liked Joelle straight away, but she didn't want to risk liking another person if that person would be taken from her, anyway. After what happened to her parents she was not willing to open her heart again.

"Would you consider adopting her?"

"We have to think about it and would like to meet with her a few more times, but we're not against it."

"Please take all the time you need and let me know what you decide when you're ready. We are still trying to get the information about her circumstances. She probably will be more eager to tell us once we have found a good family for her. You're more than welcome to spend more time with her tomorrow."

"Thank you Mrs. Carter, that is very kind."

***

"So what do you think, Jo?" Josh knew her answer, but wanted to hear the words from her mouth.

They left the orphanage and walked towards the park.

"She is a wonderful child. I had a hard time reading her mind, but I think she likes me. There is so much love and potential in her. She will do well if we find a good home for her."

Josh smiled. "The question is, where do we find a family for her?"

Joelle wandered off in her thoughts, watching people that walked past them. Jade and Crystal appeared, following a young woman running through the park.

They stopped for a short blether, as they called it in Scottish, and off they went again.

Josh watched Jo. He knew her mind wouldn't rest until she had found a suitable person for Hannah. He was invisible again and together they scanned the park with their eyes since this was an area Josh was in charge of.

Three ladies walked towards them. Jo had a feeling to pay good attention to those ladies and was drawn to one in particular. They wore business suits and were off to a business lunch.

Suddenly, a young man came out of nowhere, grabbing one ladies' handbag and ran off.

Jo, knowing that this was her chance to get acquainted with these women, jumped from the bench she was sitting on, and ran after the man. She tackled him, and both fell to the ground. The thief got up outraged that a young woman had stopped him, and pulled out a knife, ready to attack.

An angel, dressed in black, appeared behind the man.

Without having to look at Josh for confirmation, Joelle knew this was an evil angel. Josh had been right she could tell right away. Not only did she feel his evil presence, but there was something about him that told her he had never been human. He was different.

"You don't stand a chance, Joelle. This thief will stab you and everyone will know you're not human. They must send you somewhere else and you won't be able to help Hannah."

He grinned at her and she had to admit she was disgusted. Not knowing how to respond without blowing her cover as an angel, she ignored him.

The thief stepped closer. The three ladies, and other people around, held their breath as they watched the scene. Someone called the police, and a few men ran closer ready to help Jo, but they were still on the other side of the park.

Jo was in full control though. She grabbed the man by his arm, kicked the knife out of his hand by using a self-defence move she had learned while living, and threw him on the ground.

Josh laughed. "Looks like Joelle isn't that easy to stab after all, eh?"

The evil angel looked at them both. He wasn't happy and disappeared.

Loud clapping was heard as the men, who came to help her, arrived and held the thief down until the police arrived.

"Well done, Miss. You sure showed this bloke."

They gave her an impressed look. Josh smiled at her, and now the three women reached them.

"Thank you so much, Miss…?"

"Oh my name is Joelle, just call me Jo."

"Thank you so much, Jo. You're a true hero."

They smiled at her. The lady with the stolen handbag shook her hand.

"My name is Ruth Smith. Would you care to join us for lunch as a small thank you?"

"Yes that would be wonderful. I would love to join you." She had responded right away, wanting to get to know Ruth, but then realised that she probably couldn't even eat normal human food.

What am I supposed to do now?

"You'll be okay, Jo. When we're visible, we can do anything a human can do. It won't be the same for you though. If you had been stabbed earlier, everyone would have known something was different about you since they can't hurt us and we don't bleed if our body gets injured. When it comes to human food, we can eat it just fine." Josh had read her thoughts and put her at ease once again.

It was good to know she could eat human food when visible.

Josh followed the group and stayed close. They went to a cafe and sat down. Joelle and Ruth got along well. While they ate, Joelle found out that Ruth was a lawyer that prosecuted child abuse cases. She was a perfect match for Hannah. She was forty-five years old, tall, slim, with dark brown hair and she was kind and friendly. She was also humorous with the right amount of serious strictness.

When they were done eating, Ruth paid the bill, and they stood to leave.

"Jo, it was such a pleasure meeting you. Would you like to join me again tomorrow?"

"Yes I would love that very much. I'm also looking for a job. I moved here, but haven't found work yet. I'm a school teacher, but open to anything."

Ruth smiled. "I'm looking for a new assistant. My assistant told me today she'll be moving to Glasgow soon. Could you please bring your Curriculum Vitae with you tomorrow?"

Joelle agreed, and they departed.

"Wow Jo, you're incredible. You meet the girl you're assigned to, and the same day you find her a potential parent and get a job? Well done!"

Josh patted her back and made it clear how proud he was of her. Plus, it was only her second day as a guardian angel, and she hadn't tried abusing her powers… yet!

***

They stayed at the park until it was dark. There wasn't much to do. People were just passing through. Nothing major happened.

However, it was Friday night and soon a group of young men appeared, shouting and bullying everyone that came close to them. They were drunk.

Josh and Joelle kept a close eye on them as a young woman jogged along the path. She had a dog with her, a little beagle, when the men stopped her.

"Oi sweetheart," one of them said to her, while checking her out with a huge grin.

"Get out of my way."

She tried to walk past them, but they surrounded her and wouldn't let her leave. The girl was scared, but knew she had to appear calm and confident.

Josh stepped closer. So did Jo. They both read the thoughts of the men and knew what they had on their minds. Nobody else was around, except her guardian angels, so they had to pay close attention.

As soon as one man grabbed the girl by the arms, her dog growled and barked. One of them kicked the dog and then they pulled the girl closer, trying to force her into the bushes and trees behind them. She screamed.

Before Josh could do anything, Joelle had made herself visible, pushed herself between the men and the girl, and moved the girl back to protect her. She was furious and upset.

"Don't you dare touch her again! Get lost!" She could hardly control her temper.

Everyone backed off startled, but then the men laughed and one of them stepped closer, trying to touch

Joelle's face. She pushed him away from her and into St. Margaret's loch behind them. It happened so fast that nobody had time to respond.

Spitting up water, the man she had pushed came up furious and wanting revenge. It was time for Josh to step in and do damage control before they found out about Jo's unnatural strength.

He jumped behind a tree, made himself visible and then stepped in front of the girls. Surprised about his sudden appearance, the men stepped back.

What's going on? The men thought. *Nobody was here a few minutes ago. Where did these two come from?*

Everybody had these questions written on their faces.

Still furious, Jo stepped forward again.

"You better take off before I lose it. Don't you dare treat another girl like that ever again!"

Josh put his hands on her shoulders, trying to calm her down.

"You blokes should leave now before we call the police."

"Why should we? There are five against you and your mad partner."

One of them grabbed Joelle, but she threw him to the ground with another one of her self-defence moves.

Four more guardian angels made themselves visible and took action. Two female angels had already called the police. The attacked girl checked her dog to make sure he was okay.

Joelle was still furious and her whole body was shaking as she held back her anger. Trying to calm herself down, she walked over to the girl and her dog.

"Are you all right? Is there anything we can do for you?"

The girl was scared, traumatised and close to tears, but not harmed.

"No, but thank you so much. I don't even want to think about what would have happened if it hadn't been for you and your partner."

"You're welcome, but don't go running alone at night anymore. It's too dangerous."

The girl nodded.

The police arrived, arrested the drunk men, and once they finished their reports everyone left.

***

Joelle walked away from the scene, still trying to calm herself down.

"Jo!" She turned around to Josh's voice, and he grabbed her and threw her over his shoulder.

"JOSH, put me down this instant. What's gotten into you?"

"You're being punished for abusing your powers and getting involved without my permission."

"What?"

He took her off his shoulder and forced her to look at him.

"Jo, you're not allowed to interfere. You can't do that. First of all, the girl's guardian angels were there. Second, those blokes have the right to be idiots."

"No Josh, they weren't just being idiots. They wanted to harm her. Didn't you hear what they were thinking?"

"I did, but we can't get involved."

"I can't sit back and just watch a crime happen. That's not in my nature."

"You've got to, Jo. That was unacceptable." He was angry now and looked her in the eyes.

"That was not unacceptable. I'm sorry if I broke the rules, but I will not pretend that nothing is happening while I'm watching it. I would have gotten involved as a human, and I will get involved now. I have my free will, too."

She was speaking angrily but used her powers to calm him down. It worked.

"Stop that, Jo. I want to be angry right now."

"Too bad for you, Mister, I've got the power, and I'm not afraid to use it."

He couldn't help but laugh. "Seriously Jo, you can't get involved."

They had made themselves invisible and sat down on the grass.

"Watch me."

"Don't be so stubborn."

"I'm not stubborn, just rational. There is no way I will ever stop myself from helping a person when that person will get hurt or abused. I mean they were going to sexually assault her. Have you ever sat back and watched a crime like that happen?"

"No, but...."

"See?!"

"Jo, that's only because every time I've been in a situation like that, I was with someone in training and they got involved."

"Have you ever heard of other angels just watching something like that happen?"

"No I haven't...."

As he thought about it more, he had to admit that she made sense.

"Maybe you have a point there," he said. *Have I misunderstood the rules even though I've been an angel for so long?*

What a huge eye opener. He realised that terrible things only happened when the angels were occupied with something else and couldn't get there in time. It only happened when the evil angels attacked or had gained so much power over the humans that it was hard for the guardian angels to keep up.

The evil angels in this situation had done everything to distract the guardian angels, and he remembered seeing that there were evil angels behind the drunk men. Normally evil angels attack when they want something to happen, and they don't want the guardian angels to take control. He had seen them, but they hadn't attacked.

Why was that?

Joelle had been so focused on helping the girl she had completely shut them out. She probably hadn't even seen them. He knew new angels had a special power of protection: something that kept the evil angels at a distance. W*as there something special about Joelle, something that made the evil angels aware that she was more powerful than they were? Was she one of those angels who had a rare power?* He wasn't sure. But he would keep the thought in the back of his mind.

"I think you're right, Jo." He shared some of his thoughts with her (not the ones about her special power) and she nodded.

"That's how it is, Josh. I mean you told me we don't change the way we are, and how we feel when we die. Heavenly Father wants us to be ourselves because we are the way we are for a reason." She looked at him with her blue eyes and smiled.

"I can't pretend to be someone else and look the other way. It's one thing if nature takes over and it's time for people to pass away through accident or illness, but I will let no one hurt someone else while I'm around and can do something about it. I would have gotten involved as a human even if I would have been in danger myself."

"I believe it. Your sense of fairness is stronger than your sense of safety."

"True, that's how I died. Good thing I can't die anymore," she said as she winked at him.

He grinned from ear to ear, jumped to his feet and pulled her to her feet as well. It was time to go home and get a well-deserved rest.

***

Josh and Joelle reached headquarters, and said goodnight to each other. Before Joelle could open the door to her flat, Paul appeared out of nowhere, followed by Sydney.

"Hello, beautiful."

"My name is Joelle, Paul!"

"Did you have a nice day?"

Joelle smiled politely. "Yes I did, thank you."

"I heard you beat up some blokes at the park today. That's my girl."

He put his arm around her shoulders, but she removed it right away.

"Paul, I'm not your girl and if you don't stop invading my personal space, I will beat you up too."

Josh turned around. Sydney winked at him, and the next moment Jade and Crystal appeared.

Paul laughed.

"Oh you're so funny, sweetheart. I know you're strong, but face it, I'm a man and still stronger than you."

Again he tried to put his arm around her shoulders, still laughing, but she grabbed his arm and threw him over her shoulder onto the floor. The look on his face was priceless.

"Looks like you're not so strong after all, eh sweetheart?" Joelle said imitating his voice, and walked into her flat followed by Jade, Crystal and Sydney who couldn't stop giggling.

Josh snapped his fingers and disappeared laughing. The only one left was Paul lying shocked on the floor.

***

"I think she likes me," Paul remarked after he had overcome his trauma. He joined his roommate and tried starting a conversation, but Josh just wanted to rest after this long day.

"Paul, I wouldn't get my hopes up."

"Why not? Isn't it obvious? She gets defensive and angry when I'm around. That's got to mean that she loves me, but doesn't want to show it in front of everyone."

"Paul...."

"Or she feels like she shouldn't have a crush on someone now that she's an angel?"

Josh couldn't imagine that Paul believed what he told himself.

"Paul! Let me be clear with you today. Joelle has no interest in you. She feels annoyed by you and doesn't appreciate that you're constantly trying to make passes at her. She's not someone who pretends. Joelle means what she says."

Paul looked at his roommate for a second, and then raised an eyebrow in a disgusted way.

"You don't even know what you're talking about, and you don't understand women at all."

He laid down on his bed, and Josh who was lying in his own bed, turned away from him.

"Oh and you do, eh?" Josh muttered under his breath before he closed his eyes to sink into his memories.

4. She's Gone. Now What?

When Joelle and Josh entered the orphanage the next day, they were told that Hannah had escaped once again.

"I am sorry, Mr. and Mrs. McIntosh. Hannah is difficult and keeps running away. Would you like to see other children?"

"No, thank you, Mrs. Carter. We have our hearts set on Hannah. Just let us know when she comes back or has been found again." Joelle smiled at the older woman and she and Josh left the building.

Outside, Joelle turned to her trainer.

"So what are we going to do now, and how will we find her?"

"That isn't difficult, Jo. Even though we're in charge of Hannah's wellbeing, any angel will look out for her when she's around them. Let me ask where she is."

He concentrated and sent a mind message to the angels in town. Within seconds he heard from Jade, telling him where Hannah was.

"She's in a cottage near the park."

"How do you know?" Joelle gave him a puzzled look.

"Once we're fully trained, we gain another power. We can send messages, to other angels, through our thoughts."

"Wow! That is super cool."

He smiled. "It sure is. Jade responded and told me she and Crystal have been watching the girl all morning. The cottage belonged to her parents and has not been sold yet. Hannah's lawyer tried selling it, but the Guardian Angel Agency here in Edinburgh agreed to keep that from happening. That way Hannah has a place where she can hide and feel safe until we find her a home."

"How do you keep that from happening?"

"We make the humans believe it's haunted."

"What?" Joelle thought she hadn't heard him correctly.

"Whenever someone is interested in the house, two or more of us go in, turn the lights on and off, drop things, close doors...."

Joelle's eyes lit up. "That's cruel Josh. Funny, but cruel."

"Well it won't be forever, just until Hannah has a happy home."

Joelle couldn't help but laugh at the thought of the whole haunting thing.

"I bet that freaks out the humans."

"Oh yes it does. It's a very effective way to keep the house safe." He winked at her and grinned.

They walked towards the park and were met by Jade and Crystal.

"Glad you can take over. Our human is getting ready to leave the area. You're right on time. Oh and Hannah is in the garden."

"Perfect," Josh smiled. He told Joelle to make herself visible, and she walked around the house, opened the gate and stepped into the garden.

***

Hannah was sitting on a couch outside, enjoying the sunlight. When she noticed Joelle, she jumped up.

"How did you get here and how did you find me?"

Joelle smiled. "I'm surprised to see you too. I saw the - For sale - sign out front and wanted to look at the garden before contacting the owner.

Hannah looked upset and angry.

"There is no owner. This is my parent's place."

"I'm sorry, Hannah. I wasn't trying to make you uncomfortable. Do you mind if I sit down?" Hannah, not knowing what to think or say, nodded.

"Your parents had great taste. What a beautiful home. I bet you loved living here."

Tears filled the girl's eyes and Joelle moved closer, putting her arm around Hannah's shoulders. Hannah let her and Josh was again impressed.

"I didn't live here. My parents and I had a house in London, and this was our holiday home. After my parents died, I was placed in one orphanage in London, but I couldn't handle it, ran away, and came here."

"Wow, Hannah that must have been quite an adventure."

"It was. The police caught me a few times and kept putting me into orphanages, but I escaped each time."

"Does anyone here know you and this cottage belong together?"

"No, I have told no one. Our lawyer back home has tried selling the property a few times, but has had no luck."

Joelle nodded. "How have you been able to survive without money?"

"Well, I have a credit card. My daddy taught me how to use it when I was ten. He wrote in his will that my parent's money would be transferred to my account with their death."

Joelle was impressed. What a great idea to make sure your children are well taken care of.

"Why didn't your parents assign someone to take care of you in case they passed?"

"Oh they did. I was supposed to live with mummy's best friend and husband, but they were in the car too during the accident and died. You will not tell on me, right?" Hannah realised that she had opened up to Joelle and took herself back.

"No of course not, but would you mind if I popped in now and then?"

"That would be nice."

"We could even find a nice family for you, if you'd like. But one you choose, not a family chosen for you?"

Joelle used her words carefully and held her breath. *Did I go too far?*

Hannah thought about it. "Yes maybe."

Hannah's eyes looked suspicious now.

"So how did you find me? And don't tell me you were looking into buying a home. I know you were looking for me. Something in my heart tells me so. Are you in the Security Service or something?"

Joelle smiled. "Kind of I guess. I am an agent, just not for the Security Service." She looked at Josh, not knowing how to continue and he gave her a reassuring smile. "We call ourselves the Guardian Angels Agency and I'm trying to find and help kids who are lost or have run away from home. I'm not trying to take you back to the orphanage," she said after seeing Hannah's thoughts.

"I'm just making sure you're safe and okay."

Hannah felt relieved, and for some reason she trusted Joelle. Experience had taught her not to trust anyone, but there was something different about Joelle.

They had been talking for a while when Joelle noticed the time.

"Oh dear I have to go. I'm meeting someone for lunch today. She's offering me a job."

Hannah looked disappointed and lost.

"Say, would you care to join me?"

Hannah gave her a surprised look.

"Don't worry, I'll tell her you're my niece visiting for the summer."

Hannah was once again hesitant. Could she truly trust Joelle? Her heart told her yes.

"I would love that," Hannah said as she smiled at Joelle and off they went.

***

Ruth Smith had gone through tough times. First, her husband of twenty-five years had passed away after suffering a heart attack. A few months later, both her parents died of old age and her best friend moved to Australia to be with her mother who was getting on in years. Never being blessed with children, Ruth felt lonelier than ever. She worked more than ever, not letting anyone come close to her. The few friends she had didn't stick around either, and her heart was broken over and over.

However, she had met no one like Joelle before. From the moment Joelle introduced herself, Ruth felt a special bond to her. Joelle was so giving and cheerful, something she needed at this time. Ruth heart was healing.

***

Ruth Smith was surprised when Joelle showed up with a young girl, but didn't object.

Jo introduced Hannah to Ruth and asked if it was okay if Hannah joined them. Ruth had no complaints, especially since Hannah was silent and didn't say a word during the whole conversation.

Eventually Ruth turned to Hannah.

"So how do you like Edinburgh, Hannah?"

"I love it."

Ruth had to admit that she liked this girl and Joelle. It was strange that after being so occupied with her own life, not wanting to make friends, just working all day long, she now felt drawn to these two girls. This new feeling of wanting to spend private time with them surprised her. *Maybe this was her new start?*

"Jo and Hannah. I have a cottage in Drumnadrochit, not that far from Inverness, and I was wondering if you two would like to join me for a weekend trip? It's right next to Loch Ness and an exquisite area."

Ruth couldn't believe she said it out loud. *What am I doing?*

Joelle looked at Hannah and smiled.

"That sounds like fun. We would love to join you." Joelle's eyes sparkled with excitement, and she smiled a big smile at Hannah who also looked excited.

"How about Friday in a fortnight?" Again Ruth was scared at her own words. *I hardly know these two and I'm inviting them into my life? I don't even know if I can trust them.*

Joelle felt and heard the turmoil in Ruth's head. She looked deep into her eyes and calmed her down at once.

"Yes, we would be delighted," Joelle said, giving her a reassuring smile.

Ruth knew everything would be okay, and that she could trust Joelle.

"Wonderful. And please work as my assistant, Joelle. Since my current assistant won't be leaving for a couple weeks, you can start after our little weekend trip."

"Perfect, thank you," Joelle said smiling. She felt thrilled and excited, like she was bursting with energy.

They said goodbye to each other, and Ruth went back to her office.

Joelle and Hannah walked back to the cottage.

Hannah's eyes smiled with excitement for the first time since Joelle had met her.

"Mrs. Smith is a nice person, isn't she, Jo?"

"She sure is. I'm looking forward to our little trip. I'm sure it will be fun."

Joelle smiled and grabbed Hannah's hands and twirled around with her. Josh stood back and watched the two girls having fun and enjoying life. They went back to the cottage, played games together, Joelle cooked something for Hannah, and then it was time to go.

"Are you sure you will be okay during the night?"

"Of course I am, Jo. I've been doing this for months now. I trust that my guardian angels will watch over me."

Joelle winced when Hannah mentioned her guardian angels but gained control right away.

"Maybe tomorrow we can spend time together again?" Jo asked, looking at Hannah nervously, but the girl smiled and threw herself into the arms of her new friend.

"That would be brilliant. But isn't your husband home?"

"Oh yes, you're right. But I could bring him along if that's okay?"

Hannah hesitated for a moment. "He won't tell on me, right?"

"Of course not, Hannah. He's an agent too and knows when not to get involved or interfere." She gave Hannah a reassuring smile, hugged her again and left.

Hannah locked the door and was happy for the first time since her parents had died.

Joelle made herself invisible and went back into the house, looking down at the sweet child as she watched a movie.

Josh stepped closer and put his arm around Jo.

"She'll be okay. We can stay here until our shift is up. She'll then be under the care of the night shift."

Jo nodded and leaned her head against his strong shoulder.

"She is such a wonderful child. Ruth is perfect for her."

"I agree, Jo. You've done a wonderful job bringing them together. While you were playing around with Hannah, I got information from Ruth's guardian angels.

They said this was the first time in many months that she has shown any signs of opening up. After her husband and parents passed away last year, and her best friend moved to Australia, she became obsessed with her job. She's had lunch with colleagues every so often, but she doesn't socialise with anyone anymore."

"That's so sad. She's such a loving person, I can tell. We need to get her out there again."

"I agree. And it's obvious that you are the best angel to make that happen."

"But won't Ruth's angels get angry and upset at me if I take over?"

"No, because they're only assigned to protect her. They don't have a special assignment for her right now since she hasn't been willing to accept anyone into her life."

They sat down on the ground, watching Hannah with her movie.

"How did you die Josh, and how old were you?"

The question came so suddenly, but he had been expecting it.

"I was eighteen when I died. I had cancer, and even though I went through months of chemotherapy and radiation, it killed me in the end."

"I'm sorry, Josh. That must have been hard for your family, and for you."

"It was. It broke my mother's heart since I was their only child. She had depression pretty badly after my death, and when my dad couldn't handle it anymore they got divorced, which made my mum even more depressed."

"Why would your dad leave her at a time like that?" Joelle asked with a look of shock.

"She pushed him away. He couldn't handle it anymore, first losing his only child and then being pushed away by his wife. His heart was broken, too."

Josh shook his head still grieving about his past.

"What happened to your mum?"

"My uncle found her dead one day. She had taken too many pills."

He looked sad and Joelle put her arms around his neck.

"I'm sorry, Josh." He hugged her back, grateful for her comforting kindness.

"Thanks, Jo. I wish she wouldn't have given up like that. It caused those left behind great heartache, and for her as well when she arrived in heaven. Life is a precious gift from God and shouldn't be treated so lightly."

"Have you seen her since?"

"Oh yes. I was there when she died, and I greeted her when she arrived in heaven."

"That's wonderful. What is your mother doing now?"

"She was taught by the post-mortality team for a while and fell in love with one angel who was teaching her. Since he had never been married before and his feelings were mutual, they got married and are now angels assigned to heaven," he said smiling.

"What a great end to such a tragic story. Is your dad still alive?"

"Yes, he lives in Montana with his new wife and two kids. He is much happier."

"Cancer is a terrible illness. My grandfather passed away from cancer and I had other friends and relatives who didn't survive. The one thing that made it bearable for me, was my faith. Knowing we will see our loved ones again, made such a difference. I love that Heavenly Father created a way for us so we can be with our families forever. Being sealed to my family for time and all eternity, even if I am not married myself, makes me happy."

"I agree, Jo, and who knows you might even find your future companion sometime in the future and get sealed to him too." He smiled at her and looked deep into her blue eyes.

She blushed a little, but then nodded.

"Yes, maybe. I feel bad for those who lose someone and don't have the same knowledge we do, or don't believe in life after death. It has to be devastating to think they will never see their loved ones again. I wish I could help them understand."

Josh looked at her with one of his winning smiles.

"You're a wonderful person, Jo. People will know what we know if they listen to their hearts and search for the answers."

"That's true."

It was late, and time to go back to headquarters.

Hannah had fallen asleep on the couch and the night shift guardian angels were waiting outside. Jo gave Hannah a kiss on the forehead, and off they went.

***

The next day they picked up Hannah and went to church with her. Afterwards they returned to the cottage to spend the rest of the day with her.

They played board games, watched movies together and Hannah got increasingly comfortable around Joelle and Josh.

"I'm so glad we became friends, Jo. I feel happy and my life is great again." Hannah hugged her guardian angel spontaneously and smiled at her.

Joelle held her in her arms and looked at Josh who smiled too.

Reading Joelle's mind, Josh grabbed her by her hand, pulled her closer and threw her over his shoulder.

"Josh let me down this instant! What's wrong with you?"

Hannah laughed as she watched the two adults tease each other. The next moment, and before Joelle could do anything, he carried her to the little pool and threw her in.

Joelle came up spitting water, shaking her fist at him.

"You're so dead Josh McIntosh. I promise I'll get you back."

He laughed out loud, but one second later, he was in the pool too. Surprised, he looked at Hannah who had given him a big push. Then they laughed.

Hannah was happy when she fell asleep that night. She would have wonderful dreams for the first time in months.

***

"Why in the world did you throw me in the pool, Josh?" Joelle asked on their way home.

A huge grin appeared on his face that made her smile too, and she elbowed his stomach.

"Ouch!" he said and laughed.

"You better tell me, Mister!" She looked determined.

"Or else what?" He knew how to push her buttons.

"Or I must use my powers on you!"

She stepped in front of him, looking straight into his eyes, but he grabbed her again and threw her over his shoulder.

"Why do you keep doing that?" She heard other angels laughing and blushed. "Please put me down."

He took her of his shoulder, looked into her eyes and said: "I keep doing that to show you who's boss."

Again he smiled, and she elbowed him again.

"Whatever."

"For your information I threw you in the pool because I saw your thoughts and knew you wanted to tell Hannah who you are. I made sure that didn't happen."

She looked up to him, feeling guilty about what she had been thinking.

"We can't do that, Jo. I know you love the little girl, but you can't tell her who you are."

"But what am I going to do when this year of training is over and I go somewhere else? Will I just disappear from her life?"

Joelle thought her heart would break just at the thought.

"No, you'll tell her that your agency needs you somewhere else."

She couldn't help but feel sad about it.

"Don't worry, your new assignment will keep you just as occupied, happy and busy. Unfortunately goodbyes are part of being a guardian angel."

5.   Why Josh, Why?

The next two weeks went by quickly and Hannah and Joelle spent lots of time together. Josh joined them "officially" on Sundays, but was invisible the other six days. They met with Ruth often, and their friendship grew as well.

When Friday came, Hannah and Joelle were both hyper and excited. They looked forward to their upcoming little adventure and couldn't wait to see Loch Ness and the Highlands.

Unfortunately, the evil angels knew about their trip as well.

After ten miles into their journey, Joelle noticed two male angels dressed in black, hovering outside the moving car. They grinned at the guardian angels and kept following the car, getting closer and closer.

Joelle gave Josh a worried look. He told her to stay calm and not do anything. He left the car and attacked one angel while Ruth's guardian angels made sure that both Hannah and Ruth were protected as much as possible.

The second evil angel did something to the tyres, and two of them exploded. The car spun and crashed into the motorway divider wall.

The impact was so severe that both Hannah and Ruth were injured and unconscious. Other drivers stopped their vehicles, called in the accident to the police, and rushed over to help.

Joelle knew she couldn't talk to Josh now, since he was invisible, so she thought her questions in her head.

Did you know this would happen, Josh? She asked looking at him sad, upset and unhappy, and it pained him to see her this way.

He slipped back into the car.

"Yes, I knew."

Why didn't you tell me?

"Because I know how much you love Hannah and that you would have tried to protect her, maybe even blowing your cover as an angel."

Why were those evil angels trying to stop us?

"They don't want us to succeed. They want Hannah and Ruth to be miserable. They hope by putting obstacles in our way, we won't be able to make a family out of them."

Joelle watched three men trying to open her door while others tried to get to Hannah and Ruth. When they opened Joelle's door, they were surprised that she wasn't hurt.

"Are you okay, Miss?"

"Yes, I'm fine, thank you." She wanted to be with Hannah, but had to stay in her human-like body and couldn't do anything.

She looked so sad and disappointed.

She wanted to get out of the car, but the men who had opened her door told her to stay put. They would carry her out. Knowing she couldn't tell them the truth she nodded, continued to act human, and pretended to be in shock.

Some helpers carefully carried her to the side of the road and helped her sit down. Josh sat next to her.

Why did this have to happen? Will Ruth or Hannah die? She looked into his direction and he looked deep into her eyes, calming her down at once.

"No, they won't. It had to happen to test them. It's a trial for both. The evil angels don't want us to succeed. They will keep putting obstacles in our way, hoping we will give up." He took her head into his hands and gave her a kiss on the forehead.

She sighed. *They will never stop us, Josh. They can kiss my bum for all I care, but those evil angels will not make me give up. I'm stubborn for a reason, and will show them how stubborn I can be.*

He smiled at Ruth's guardian angels and they smiled back. Hannah and Ruth were in good hands as long as Joelle was around.

Finally the ambulance and fire brigade arrived too.

They got Hannah out of the car, and Joelle was by her side right away. She held her hand and was with her when she was lifted into the ambulance.

Removing Ruth out of the car was harder. Ruth was stuck underneath the steering wheel and the firemen had to cut her out. Once they rescued her, they put her in the ambulance as well and took both to the hospital in Edinburgh.

Hannah and Ruth were still unconscious when they arrived and that worried everyone a great deal.

***

"Are you a relative?" a big nurse asked abruptly as she stopped Joelle who was trying to follow Hannah into the examining room.

"No, but...."

"Then you can't come in here."

"But I'm a close friend."

"You can't come in here, sorry," she said and closed the door in Joelle's face.

Joelle stepped back, angry and upset.

Another nurse addressed her. "What is your relationship with the girl?"

"We are friends."

"What's her name?"

"Hannah."

"And last name?"

Joelle looked at Josh with terror in her eyes. She didn't even know Hannah's last name.

"Spencer is her last name."

Thank you.

He smiled at her. "You're doing a great job using your thoughts to communicate with me."

She gave him another thankful look and looked back at the nurse, pretending to be confused.

"Forgive me, what was your last question?"

"What is Hannah's last name?"

"Spencer."

"Where are the girl's parents and how can we notify them?"

"Her parents died in a car accident last year. My friend Ruth and I were taking her on this trip before going back to the orphanage."

The nurse wasn't sure what to do or what to think. Joelle was worried when she read the nurse's thoughts:

Why hadn't they taken her to the orphanage? If they were her guardians, there would be no need to take her to the orphanage. Should I contact the police so they can investigate? Had they taken the child without someone's consent, or were they trying to blackmail the parents for money?

The nurse looked at Joelle, and Jo stared at her, calming her down at once.

Once Joelle told the nurse everything she knew, and after Joelle had left the reception desk, another guardian angel stepped up to the nurse and erased her memory of Ruth and Joelle.

She took Joelle's and Ruth's information off the computer so both wouldn't get in trouble later on. The angel left Hannah's full name, that she had been injured in a car accident, and the information about the orphanage. Everything else was gone.

Joelle felt tired after giving the nurse the information she needed. She sat down in a chair, hoping for news about Hannah.

Josh sat next to her, putting his arm around her shoulders.

Can't you go into the room and find out what is going on? She thought.

"She will be fine. We're outside our territory right now and I can't go in there. This place is full of guardian angels, and they don't like it when we take over."

What do you mean by 'we're outside our territory right now'? Don't they belong to the same agency we do? Joelle was confused; this didn't make any sense.

"The hospital is a special place with special guardian angels. They're always here: calming down patients, relatives and friends; guiding people from life into death; being there for the doctors and nurses...."

And sure enough, when Joelle lifted her head, four angels flew through the corridor. One of them waved at her, letting her know everything would be fine.

Does that mean the hospital is their headquarters and their working place?

"Yes."

Is that the same for the orphanage? Why we didn't stay there before Hannah ran away? Josh smiled at her. She was very aware of her surroundings.

"Yes the orphanage is another special guardian angel headquarter, the nursing home is too."

Why didn't I see any angels when we visited Hannah at the orphanage?

"They stay out of our way and don't show themselves when we have an assignment. But they take over when we leave."

Joelle was impressed how well this whole guardian angel system worked and that everyone was well taken care of.

So the only time humans are not protected, or in real danger, is when their time is up or evil angels distract or attack us?

"Correct."

Josh was very proud of his new trainee. She was grasping things quickly. She also showed she was ready to move on to the next challenge now that she realised everything happens for a reason and has a purpose.

Do you know what's going on with Ruth?

"She's having an operation right now. She had internal bleeding, and they needed to take care of it."

Joelle sank deeper into her seat.

Why couldn't we have stopped it?

"Sometimes all we can do is be there for those we care about. We can't interfere with anyone's free will whether they are human or angels."

Is that why you didn't use your calming powers when those blokes in the park attacked the girl?

"Yes that's why."

The door opened, and a doctor stepped out. Joelle jumped up.

"Is Hannah going to be okay?"

"Yes she will be fine. She's awake and is asking for you. She has a concussion, and a broken arm, but otherwise is a very lucky girl."

"Can I go in to see her now?"

"Yes, but don't stay too long."

The doctor left and Joelle walked into the room.

Seeing Hannah so lifeless on a hospital bed was a shock, but she walked over to Hannah's bed, gently touching her hand.

Hannah opened her eyes, looking at Joelle with a smile. Then her head sank to the side, and she was asleep. A nurse came in and addressed Joelle.

"Sorry but you have to leave now. Since you're not a relative, you can't stay here overnight, but you may come back tomorrow morning."

Joelle nodded, kissed Hannah's forehead and left the room.

Can't we stay here if I make myself invisible?

She looked at Josh, but before he could answer, two young angels appeared out of nowhere.

"Hannah will be fine. We will stay with her during the night and let you know if anything happens. Also, Ruth is in the intensive-care unit now. Her operation went well and she will be okay too. You won't be able to see her, but she's being well taken care of." The angel smiled at her, and Josh took Jo's hand.

"She'll be okay." He snapped his fingers and the next moment they were at the GAA office on High Street.

***

Joelle dropped herself into a seat.

"What will happen to Hannah when she's better?"

"They'll release her from the hospital and send her to the orphanage."

"Can't we stop them?"

"No, we can't interfere, Jo, but I'm sure Hannah will escape again and we can continue to befriend her until Ruth is ready to adopt her."

There was a loud swooshing sound, and Sydney and Paul appeared in the room.

The last person Joelle wanted to see was Paul. She didn't feel like dealing with him and his madness. She wanted to relax and stood up to leave. Before she could do anything, the insane angel was next to her.

"Oi beautiful, are you okay? I heard you blokes were in an accident and the little lass you look after got hurt. I bet you feel awful that you failed and weren't able to do your job."

"Paul!" Sydney gave her partner a warning look. He ignored her.

"It happens to the best of us my love!"

"For the last time, Paul, my name is Joelle and I am not your love!" Joelle looked upset and breathed through her teeth.

"I understand that you are frustrated with yourself, sweetie. I would feel that way too if I had let my human down!" Paul smiled at her in a pitiful way.

Joelle looked at him stunned. How could anyone be so insensitive and rude? Before she could respond, Josh got up, angry.

"Be quiet, Paul. Just leave her alone, okay?"

"I'm trying to make her feel better."

"Yeah, well you suck at it. If that's how you make people feel better, then you better keep your mouth shut in the future." Josh had never been so harsh. Sydney, and even Joelle, had to hide their smiles.

"Well Josh, I wasn't talking to you."

Paul passed him and walked up next to Joelle.

"Anything I can do for you, sweetie?"

"Yes! Stop calling me sweetie and leave me alone."

"Come on, Jo. When I feel down, it always helps when someone lifts me up. And I'd do anything for you, sweetheart." He winked at her smiling.

"Yeah? Well guess what Paul, you are not uplifting. Your comments are unnecessary and unwelcome."

She stared at him, wondering why he couldn't respect her wish for privacy.

Instead of leaving her to herself, he stepped closer and tried to give her a hug, but she shoved him away from her.

"ENOUGH, Paul. I'm so sick of this. I don't understand why you think I'm interested in you in any way. I'm not, I can assure you. Just leave me alone and stop hugging me without my consent."

"So you are okay with Josh hugging you, but you have a problem with me? What gives him the right to do something like that and you expect me to stay away?"

"Josh isn't hitting on me and trying to get me on a date. He's acting like a friend."

"Sure he is." She heard the sarcasm in his voice but before she could respond, he beamed another smile at her. "The only reason you get so angry at me is because you're scared of your own feelings. Just admit you feel attracted to me."

"You can't be serious! Listen, Paul. I'm not interested."

"I don't believe that," he said shaking his head. "I have never accepted 'no' as an answer as a human, and will not start now. Why are you playing hard to get?"

Joelle, Josh and Sydney were speechless for a moment. All three of them couldn't believe what they had just heard.

Jo was beyond furious now though, and her eyes flashed at him angrily.

"How Dare You! How dare you accuse me of playing hard to get! You have no right to judge me like that. You are a tosser, Paul! You don't take 'no' for an answer? Who do you think you are? You are not superior to me, or any girl, and don't get to decide who we want to be with. Maybe it is time for you to learn that no means no!!! I can't play hard to get because I wasn't playing. I have no feelings for you, and that will not change no matter how entitled you think you are. You should respect us women, and stop being so selfish!"

Paul looked hurt at her outburst, but he was too absorbed in himself to just let it go.

When she turned around, wanting to leave the room, he grabbed her arm.

"Jo..."

"Don't touch me!" She snapped, looking so angry he let go at once. "You don't get it do you, Paul? Read my lips if you can't hear the words coming out of my mouth. I'm not in love with you, I'm not attracted to you and we will never, ever be a couple. You're annoying, nothing else, so stop thinking I'm in any way interested in you. If you want to be friends, be my friend, but keep your distance."

He stepped back and was very offended.

"I'm sorry I had to hurt you, Paul, but I don't think you would have gotten the message any other way."

She said goodnight to everyone and disappeared.

Josh, Sydney and Paul followed her lead and went to their flats.

6. Healing Time

Josh waited for Joelle when she appeared in the office the next morning. He sat in one of the black leather seats next to the window.

"Good morning, Josh."

"Good morning, Jo." He got up and gave her a hug.

"You look serious, did something happen?"

She looked alarmed and realised what must have happened.

"Did Paul give you a hard time?"

He nodded, and they both sat down.

"Paul went on and on how you misunderstood him and how he tried to welcome you. He thinks you're so ungrateful, and mean, and that he doesn't deserve to be treated that way."

Joelle was shocked that Paul twisted everything around and was now trying to blame her. She had to admit she had been harsh the night before, but he was the one who constantly made her uncomfortable by making passes at her. Even after she had let him know repeatedly that she wasn't interested, he kept pestering her.

"Jo, don't worry. He'll come around with time. Sydney and Jade had to do the same thing. After a while he stopped being offended and moved on to the next person." Josh had read her mind.

She got up and looked out the window, watching humans walk past the building. Eventually she turned around.

"He can't possibly think his hitting on me could be misunderstood. It was so obvious, and I tried letting him know every single time. What was I supposed to do, pretend I liked him too so I wouldn't hurt his feelings?" Joelle asked with an angry look on her face.

Josh got up too and looked into her eyes.

"You did nothing wrong, Jo. He brought this on himself, and he will understand that with time."

Sighing she looked passed him to the door. "I hope you're right."

***

The hospital was busier than the day before, and this time Joelle noticed how many angels were there. Every room and corridor had angels hovering around inside.

She felt grateful since that meant the people who were ill or dying were being well taken care of.

Josh made himself visible, and together they entered Hannah's room. She ate something and looked better than she did the night before.

"Hello Hannah, how are you doing?" Josh asked as he sat next to her and shook her healthy hand.

"I'm doing well, thanks, Josh. How are you, Jo? Did you get hurt?"

Her eyes moved toward her angel friend and Jo smiled at her.

"I'm fine. I was lucky and didn't get hurt."

"Looks like our guardian angels were busy keeping us safe," Hannah said smiling.

Knowing what was going on in Joelle's head, Josh took her hand and squeezed it gently, to remind her not to say anything she shouldn't.

She gave him a cheeky look and thought: *Don't worry; I will not tell her who we are. There's no need for you to throw me over your shoulder.*

He coughed to hide his huge grin, and they sat with Hannah until she fell asleep.

When the two angels stepped out of the room, one of the guardian angels in the corridor stopped in front of them.

"Ruth is in a regular room now. She can have visitors." Josh and Joelle exchanged a look.

Where can we find her?

"She is in ward three, room two seventy four."
Thank you. Josh smiled and the angel left.

***

Ruth had her eyes closed when Joelle and Josh entered the room. It was a bright and friendly room with large windows, light green walls and matching curtains. Ruth wasn't alone in the room. There was another bed occupied by an old woman who had trouble breathing.

Two female angels sat next to the elderly woman, stroking her arms. Joelle heard them whisper to each other.

"How much longer do you think before she passes on?"

"Not much longer."

"It's so sad that none of her children are here, even after each was contacted by the doctor a few days ago." The second angel agreed.

Joelle couldn't stop looking at the woman. She was probably eighty years old. Her wrinkly face had no life in it. Her hands were worn, and she had a bitter-sad smile on her face.

One angel looked at Joelle, reading the questions in her mind.

"The woman's husband passed away twenty years ago. Her children hardly visit, and she'll be dead within the next few minutes."

Jo gave Josh a sad look, and he put his arm around her shoulders.

Why didn't her children come to be with her during her final hour?

The second angel responded this time. She was young looking, a beautiful girl with long black hair and friendly loving eyes.

"They're too busy with work and making sure their careers are doing well. This woman is my grandmother."

How did you die?

"I died five years ago in a fire. I was only ten. My parents were always either working or out partying, and one night a defective night lamp exploded and caused a fire. I was able to rescue my siblings, and was right behind them, but the house collapsed before I could reach the door."

A strange but peaceful feeling filled the room as the woman's heart rate dropped, causing many alarms to go off including the heart monitor. The loud and frightening noises woke up Ruth who looked around confused, not seeing Joelle since Josh stood in the way.

Everyone's eyes were glued to the older woman whose body was giving up.

Doctors and nurses came running into the room shouting instructions at each other, trying to revive her.

The young angel kissed her grandmother's hand.

"It's almost over, Gran. You're almost there. Granddad is waiting on the other side."

Joelle had tears in her eyes watching this scene, hearing the last words of this brave young angel. They saw the elderly woman's spirit leave her body, give a thankful look to her granddaughter and the other angels in the room, and was gone.

The older angel looked one doctor in the eyes, calming him down and letting him know it was over.

"That's enough. She's gone. Time of death...," he said looking at his watch, "...11:45am."

They removed the tubes and instruments, covered the body with a bed sheet and moved her out of the room. Her two guardian angels disappeared.

Joelle had to calm herself before turning to Ruth who had witnessed everything with her human eyes but had felt a strange peaceful feeling.

Josh looked into Joelle's eyes, kissing her forehead before she could face reality again.

"Jo, when did you get here?" Ruth asked when she recognised Joelle.

"I was here the whole time and saw what happened."

"It was sad, but there was such a peaceful, wonderful feeling. It was as if a spiritual being was with the woman guiding her to the other side," Ruth remarked.

Joelle smiled. "I felt it too."

Ruth leaned back feeling tired, but still thinking about the special feeling she had felt. She hadn't felt this peaceful when her parents or husband passed away. She wondered if there were angels, guiding humans to the other world? She was lost in thought when Joelle, who read her mind, addressed her again.

"Oh Ruth, this is my husband Josh."

Ruth smiled and shook his hand.

"How are you doing, Jo? Did you get hurt in the accident? I'm so sorry it happened. How's Hannah?"

"Don't worry, Ruth. It wasn't your fault, and no I didn't get hurt. I was fortunate. Hannah has a concussion, and a broken arm, but is otherwise fine. How are you feeling?"

Ruth looked tired and in pain. She wasn't feeling well, but glad to see Jo and find out she was okay.

Ruth addressed Josh.

"Please don't blame me for the accident. I'm sorry, I didn't want this to happen."

Josh gave her a reassuring smile. "I don't blame you at all. Please don't worry. Everything's okay. It could have happened to anyone."

Still, her guilty feeling remained. Her angels stepped closer and gave her the calming look, helping her feel better about herself.

"We won't stay long today. Get some rest. We'll come and visit again tomorrow."

"Thank you for your visit, Jo, and it was nice to meet you, Josh."

"It was nice to meet you too." The two angels smiled at her and left the room.

Since nobody was in the corridor, they made themselves invisible.

"Oh Josh, that was sad and beautiful at the same time. How sad that the grandmother had to die alone. How sad that the young angel died at ten years old saving her siblings, and that she was the only one there for her grandmother. But how beautiful that she was the angel who watched over her grandmother and was there in the end. Do you know what happened to the girl's siblings?" She asked looking up at him as they walked towards the ward where Hannah was.

"After the police had spoken with the neighbours, they discovered that the children were unsupervised before the fire, and that they had been unsupervised many times. After that, they took the children away and put them into foster homes. The old woman wasn't able to take care of them, due to her age and illness, otherwise she would have raised the children."

"What a tragedy that a family had to be separated because of the parents' selfish behaviour."

Josh agreed. It was indeed sad. Both felt grateful that they had been raised in good homes and that their parents had loved them with all their hearts.

They went back to visit Hannah again and stayed until visiting hours were over.

***

After leaving the hospital they walked towards Holyrood Park to continue their duties as guardian angels until their shift was up.

They walked past a playground. Parents talked to each other, and the children played.

As a group of children played on the slide, a one-year-old toppled over the side and fell head first toward the ground. His guardian angels had been arguing with evil angels and weren't able to reach the child fast enough.

Without thinking twice, Jo jumped in, making sure the child landed softly in a pile of leaves without being injured. The child looked at her and smiled.

Startled, Joelle got up when the child's mother reached her now screaming baby, grateful that nothing bad had happened.

One of the evil angels came over to Joelle.

"You will never stop us. We will continue to make things miserable for you and we will continue to make life tough for the humans."

Joelle gave him a firm and angry glance.

"Oh is that right? We'll see who wins in the end. Love and kindness have always won over evil, and we'll work our bums off to make sure you blokes don't take over the world. I promise you that."

The evil angel gave her a dirty look and disappeared.

"Thanks Jo, good thing you and Josh were close to help," one of the child's guardian angels said as they came over, grateful that she had stepped in.

"You're right, we can't let those halfwits take over the world. We have to keep fighting the good fight," the other guardian angel said smiling as she gave Jo a nudge on the shoulder.

Once they were by themselves again, Joelle turned to Josh.

"That baby smiled at me. Can babies see us?"

"Yes, they're still close to God and as long as they can't talk, they can see and feel things other older humans can't."

***

When they reached the park, they saw the girl who had been attacked a few weeks earlier. This time she had her dog and a male friend running with her. Jo was glad she had listened to her.

Once it was dark, and Josh and Joelle were getting ready to leave the park, Marissa and Destinee appeared out of nowhere.

"Quick Josh, we need your help. Amber, the little girl we protect, is gone. We found the mum drunk in her room and then got attacked by two evil angels. After getting rid of them, Amber was gone and we have no idea where she is." Both angels looked anxious.

"Calm down, Destinee," Josh said. "Do you have any idea who might have taken the girl?"

"Most likely the mum's ex-husband. He's a drug addict, so we're not sure what he will do to her. He's beaten his daughter before, for crying too much, and she ended up in the hospital. He's upset now because when the girl's mum found out, she reported him to the police and broke up with him straight away. He's not allowed to be near them anymore and even spent time in the pound for a few months. When he got out, he wanted revenge. Now I'm worried that he has the child and will beat her to death."

Joelle couldn't help but feel horrible. They had to find the man and child before it was too late.

"How did he get into the flat?"

"I'm not sure, but Amber's mum has changed as well the past few weeks. She's been drinking more and beat her daughter as well."

Joelle looked angry. "Where are the mother's guardian angels?"

"She has evil angels around her now and they keep her guardian angels away. Marissa and I are always surrounded by evil angels and it's uncomfortable, but we don't want to leave Amber. The evil angels have threatened us, and tried kicking us out, but we've been firm. Today, however, we found the mother hammered, and when we turned around two evil angels attacked us by forcing us back into the mum's bedroom. I'm guessing the father entered during that time and took the little girl," Destinee said, close to tears.

Joelle couldn't believe what she was hearing!

"How old is Amber?"

"She's four."

Joelle was shocked and clenched her fists.

Josh got involved now.

"Do you know where the father lives?"

"I have no idea."

"Okay, let me ask around." Josh sent one of his mind messages over town, and after a few minutes he heard from Sydney and Paul.

"Sydney said they heard a child screaming and crying in a block of flats close to where they are. They said they tried to get into the building, but couldn't since evil angels are blocking the entrance."

"Okay let's go," Joelle said, determined to get the girl back.

***

When they arrived at Dungin Place, they saw the crowd of evil angels in front of the building.

"Has anyone called the police?" Josh looked at Sydney and Paul.

"We heard from one angel inside that he finally convinced his human to call the police. They've heard the beatings, screaming and crying for the past hour, but everyone around here is too scared to do anything since this is such a bad area." Paul was just as worried as everyone else.

Josh scanned the building. "Why didn't the angels inside get involved and helped?"

"They can't get out of the building, or their humans flats. It looks like the evil angels have closed the exits for the guardian angels and they're stuck. None of their powers work right now."

Joelle was furious. Something had to be done.

"If you can distract those angels, maybe I can sneak in and get the girl out."

Josh who knew there was something special about her, nodded, willing to try it out.

Sure enough, Sydney, Paul, Josh, Destinee and Marissa attacked the angels and Joelle sneaked passed them. She heard a child screaming in anguish as she entered the flat.

***

A man either high on drugs or drunk was on the phone. Joelle heard him say: "THIS is for you sending me to the pound. Now you'll never see your little girl again."

She heard a woman screaming through the phone as he hung up. Amber lifted her head and whimpered. The man shouted at her to shut up and raised his fist to hit her again.

Not being able to control herself any longer, Joelle made herself visible.

"GET AWAY FROM THAT CHILD THIS INSTANT!" She shouted at him and he stepped away startled, having trouble keeping himself standing. He stared at her, not knowing what to think, when a second man walked into the room.

"How did she get in here?" He asked confused, then smiled. "Is that the kid's mum, Robert?" Not waiting for an answer, he turned to her. "Doesn't your daughter look

113

precious now? THAT's for sending my brother to the pound."

"That's not my ex-wife," Robert mumbled.

Shocked the second man stepped closer.

"Who are you?"

Two evil angels appeared, laughing at Joelle.

Joelle was furious. Robert, still shocked that Joelle had appeared, fell backwards over the couch behind him.

His brother tried to grab Joelle, but she pushed him across the room.

"Don't you dare touch me! How can you torture an innocent little child?"

He tried to grab a knife from his pocket, but Joelle pinned him against the wall and he couldn't move. Never in his life had he seen or felt such strength. Now both men looked scared.

The little girl let out another whimper and Robert lifted his fists again. Joelle saw red, and by looking at him, she lifted him up off his feet and he flew against the wall behind him. Joelle was stunned.

The two men and evil angels had terror written on their faces. She made herself invisible again, right in front of the two scared humans.

The two evil angels, realising Joelle had more power than they, tried mocking her to hide their own worried feelings.

"She will die, Joelle. You won't be able to save her now."

Her rage got worse, and some hidden power came out and pushed the angels out of the room.

The next moment, Josh and Paul arrived and made sure the evil angels stayed outside.

Joelle turned around to face the father of the girl. She was so furious, she made herself visible again. She was about to hit him with all the anger she felt, when Josh saw what Joelle was doing. He grabbed her arm, pulled her backwards and made her invisible.

"Let me go! He deserves punishment. He brutally attacked this poor little girl."

She tried to get away from her trainer, but he grabbed her by her upper arms and held her firm.

"JO STOP! Look at me!" He said in a stern forceful voice. When she looked up, he continued softer. "You can't do that no matter how much you want to protect her. You can't attack him. We can defend ourselves against humans, and we can attack evil angels when needed, but we're not allowed to attack humans. I know it is hard but you have to accept his agency!"

He held her a little longer until he felt she had calmed down enough.

Joelle knelt next to the little girl. Tears streaming down her face, she took Amber into her arms and held her.

Her tiny little body looked terrible, blood all over. Not only had they beaten her, but must have kicked her too. The child probably had internal bleeding. They heard sirens and police officers came running up the stairs.

Josh came closer, crouched down next to Joelle and put his arm on Joelle's shoulder. Jo kissed the little girl. Just then the child let out her last breath and her spirit left her body.

Putting the body back on the ground, Joelle stood up. Amber's spirit looked at her.

"Am I dead now?"

"Yes," Joelle responded. "Nobody can hurt you anymore." The girl smiled at Joelle, gave a thankful look to Josh and Paul and disappeared.

One moment later, someone kicked the door in and officers ran inside the flat. Weapons ready to shoot, they saw both men leaning against the walls and the dead little girl.

Joelle watched everything in a blur. She couldn't understand why anyone would beat a small child to death for revenge. She couldn't understand why anyone would beat a child, period.

Outside, Marissa, Destinee, Sydney and a few other guardian angels still tried to keep the evil angels from going in. When Joelle came outside, the evil angels laughed.

"We told you, she would die. Looks like you're not as strong as you think, eh? Time to give up, Joelle."

She turned her head and gave them a cold and firm look.

"You disgust me. I will never, ever give up on making this world a better place. You might be successful in influencing some, but there will always be people that will listen to us and be on our side. You will not win. God is on our side and He is the most powerful being that exists. Sure, He will let you torture and hurt innocent people because you have your free will, but you will get what you deserve. I promise you that. Justice will get you in the end. The people who have suffered, because of your influence, will not have died in vain."

The evil angels who were mocking her before, had fear in their eyes. They gave her another dirty look and then disappeared.

***

Joelle was very quiet on the way home. Josh looked at her worried, took her hand, turned her around and looked into her eyes. She started crying, and he pulled her into his strong arms, comforting her.

"Why would anyone hurt a child like that?" She still couldn't get over it.

"The evil angels have power. They can influence humans to do evil, and when drugs and alcohol are involved, it gets even worse." He kissed her head and noticed that she calmed down.

"You showed yourself before I came in, didn't you? And you used your angel strength against those men? I saw how scared they were." She nodded.

"I couldn't stop myself. When I walked in there, and saw the child half dead on the floor, there was so much rage inside me that I didn't care anymore. I told myself that they deserved to feel scared. I wanted them to know that there is something out there, stronger and more powerful than they will ever be." He nodded.

"The evil angels are worried now. I saw fear in their eyes too when you told them off. I think they realise now you won't give up no matter how many obstacles they put in your way."

"Good, I am glad they got the message."

***

As they continued walking Joelle thought about the special power she had felt and used. She wondered if that was a coincidence or if she had another power. She knew she should ask Josh, but something stopped her. Josh didn't know of all the powers. Maybe it was best to wait and see if this happened again, or to ask Peter next time she saw him.

***

Marissa and Destinee were transferred the next day. They were both sent to a hospital in Denver, Colorado and would continue serving together.

Hannah was released a few days later. The hospital called the orphanage to make sure she made it there this time. Hannah wasn't happy, but had no choice in the matter.

One week later, Ruth was also released, eager to go back to work, but had to take it easy still. Joelle worked with Ruth and spent many hours in court fighting child abuse. It was a shocking experience when she found out how many adults abused and tortured their children.

Hannah stayed at the orphanage for a few weeks until her arm was healed. Then one night, she ran away right after supper. Jo and Josh had been watching her and went by the cottage to make sure she was okay.

***

One day during lunch, Ruth walked through the park by herself. She noticed the cottage with the "for sale" sign and stepped into the garden. Surprised she saw Hannah sitting on her favourite couch.

She jumped up when she noticed Ruth.

"Hannah, what are you doing here? Shouldn't you be in school?" Ruth asked stepping closer not knowing what to think.

"I don't go to school right now."

"And why? Does your aunt know? And what about your parents?"

"Joelle isn't my aunt." She told Ruth everything and begged her not to tell on her. "Please Ruth, let no one know. This is the only place where I feel home and safe."

Ruth was shocked, angry and confused. *Why hadn't Joelle told her this?* She looked around and had to admit that this was a beautiful place. Bushes and a white fence surrounded a cute little pool, colourful flowers, and the whole garden. Behind the bushes she saw the trees of the park. No wonder Hannah loved this place.

"You can't stay here by yourself. Is Joelle at least staying with you?"

"No, but I asked her not to. I have been on my own for a few months now and don't mind at all."

"Why didn't Joelle do anything?"

"She has been here for me all this time. I asked her not to tell anyone. She works for a secret agency trying to protect me, and is working on finding me a new home."

Ruth thought about that and then it struck her. Suddenly she knew what was going on. Joelle had lied to her and had been putting on an act the whole time. Joelle wanted her to adopt Hannah!

Ruth felt as if someone had kicked her in the stomach. She had opened up after all this time, leaving herself vulnerable; only to find out she had been lied to.

She got up and left without saying another word.

Hannah didn't know what she had said that would have hurt Ruth. She was worried and scared that Ruth might tell someone about her and the cottage.

7. Betrayal or Not?

Joelle and an invisible Josh had been doing work for Ruth, when Joelle heard Ruth come back to the office. Her new boss opened the door and slammed it shut behind her.

"How could you, Joelle? I trusted you! I opened up to you, gave you a job and all this time you've been lying about everything."

Joelle glanced at Josh, being overwhelmed by the attack. Josh put his hands on her shoulders to calm her down and to let her know he was backing her up.

"I went on a walk and found Hannah in the garden of a cottage. Is it true that Hannah is an orphan and you knew about the cottage she's been living in? Are you seriously working for some agency and have the nerve to ask me for a job too?"

"Ruth, please let me explain…."

"How dare you use me like that? You were trying to manipulate me so I would adopt Hannah, isn't that right?" She was furious and slammed her hand on her desk.

"Ruth…"

"You are such a liar, Joelle. You will regret this, I promise. I will report you and Hannah! How could you do this to me?" She looked at the angel with a sad, hurt look, turned around and left, slamming the door behind her.

One evil angel appeared, chuckling.

"I told you we would make your life miserable."

"GET OUT!" Josh snapped, shoving him so hard that the evil angel smacked through all the walls at once.

"What am I going to do, Josh? Have I done everything wrong? Should I have told her the truth about us and Hannah?"

"Calm down, Jo, everything will be fine."

"Shouldn't we go after Ruth and calm her down? I've never seen her so angry." Joelle was crushed and felt so helpless. She tried to follow the other woman, but Josh stepped in her way and grabbed her by her arms.

"We have to give her time to come to her senses."

"But what if she reports Hannah? We need to get to her before she can do something she might regret. Let me go!" She tried to loosen his hands, but he held her firm.

"Jo, you need to calm down!"

"I am calm, Josh. Just get out of my way so I can get to Ruth and explain everything."

"She won't listen to you right now. She is too upset. Let her think it over."

"How can we let her go? We are in charge of Hannah's wellbeing. We can't let Ruth tell on her. Now let go of my arms!" She became increasingly irritated.

"NO! You are too emotional right now."

"You have no right to hold me against my will. GET out of my way, Josh!" She tried pushing him away from her, but he continued to hold her firmly.

It always amused him when Joelle's temper reached a boiling point and she tried to resist him. Her stubbornness came right through here.

When he noticed that her irritation faded, he pulled her into arms and she broke out in tears. They were both invisible now, in case someone walked in.

She leaned her head against his chest and silently sobbed. It broke his heart to see her so upset, but it was something they had to go through together.

When her crying stopped, he let her go and wiped away her tears.

"Listen, Jo. You did nothing wrong. We can't tell Ruth who we are, because she wouldn't believe it anyway. And if she believed it, she would expect constant protection from us. Ruth got upset when

Hannah told her the whole story and the evil angel used that against us."

"But shouldn't we follow Ruth? What if she tells on Hannah and things get worse?"

"Ruth's guardian angels are with her now, doing damage control and probably punching the living daylight out of the evil angel," he said as he winked at Joelle and it made her smile.

"To be honest, I would love to punch that angel myself."

"I'm sure you would, I have to admit it felt good smacking him through the walls."

***

Ruth had reached the park and sat down on a bench. Her first thought was that she should go to the police and report Hannah and Joelle, but she had to calm down first. Everything tumbled around in her mind and she couldn't think clearly. Question after question….

I have to confront Joelle again to get answers. There must be a terrible mistake. Joelle doesn't seem like someone who would knowingly hurt and use someone.

She relaxed and her angels used the moment to stare into her eyes and help her feel better.

The evil angel tried to get involved again, but this time both guardian angels were in control. They put a protective shield around her so the evil angel couldn't come close again. He vanished angrily.

When Ruth stepped into her office again, she was calm and ready to talk things through. She opened the door and sat down.

"Now tell me, Joelle. What was this about?"

Knowing that Ruth was now willing to listen to her, Joelle told her as much truth as possible.

"I work for an agency that protects children, and finds new homes for them. I met Hannah first, and when I later met you, I felt that the two of you would be a great match. I would have never used you to adopt. I wanted to give you two a chance to get to know each other and see what would happen."

Ruth had to admit it made sense, and she couldn't help but believe Joelle.

"I didn't get this job to become rich I promise. I don't work for money. Your pay cheques have gone back into your bank account."

Surprised Ruth turned on her computer, went online and sure enough, the outgoing money, had come right back in. Now she was stunned as she had seen nothing like this before.

"I had no intention of hurting you, Ruth. I wanted to improve your life by introducing Hannah to you. She is such a sweet child. Yes I allowed her to stay at the cottage, even though I knew she should be at the orphanage, but I wanted Hannah to feel safe in her present situation. I figured I'd rather have her stay at the cottage and know where she is, than have her wander around Scotland, being in constant danger."

Joelle's blue eyes stared at her and Ruth knew she was telling the truth. She took Joelle's hand and squeezed it gently.

"Thank you for being so honest with me, Jo. I understand now what you did and why you did it, and I'm sorry I was so angry earlier. I normally don't lose control, but it felt like you had betrayed me and abused my trust, and that hurt badly."

Joelle got up and hugged her.

"It's okay, Ruth." They smiled at each other.

"Does Hannah know you were hoping I would adopt her?"

"No she doesn't. When I met Hannah, I promised her I would help her find someone to choose so she would feel comfortable with the situation. But I never mentioned to her I was hoping for you."

Ruth nodded. "I have to admit I feel good about Hannah and liked her from the beginning. Please give me time to get to know her better and get myself ready in case I feel it is right for me."

"Ruth, there is no pressure and you have all the time in the world."

***

A few weeks later, Ruth surprised Joelle and Hannah with the news that she had bought the cottage. She had spent many hours thinking about it. Even though she wasn't ready to decide yet whether or not to adopt Hannah, or to move into the cottage herself, she wanted to make sure that Hannah had a place to be safe.

She had contacted Hannah's lawyer, met with him in London and had signed the contracts to make it final.

Hannah jumped into Ruth's arms and hugged her, feeling grateful.

"Thank you so much, Ruth. I have to admit I was worried you would tell on me, but I'm glad I was wrong. This is the most wonderful surprise ever."

Ruth hugged her back with a smile.

"I knew it was the right thing to do. I don't like the thought of you living here by yourself, but I want you to feel safe. I know Jo and Josh will look after you."

Jo stepped closer too and hugged Ruth with gratefulness.

"Now that I've bought a cottage, I feel like we need to celebrate. How about we make something special for supper tonight?"

Ruth was happy and excited. She went to the shop to get the ingredients for Haggis, neeps and tatties, and they had a wonderful evening together. After finishing the meal with delicious custard for dessert, she had another surprise for them.

"I decided that we should try our Loch Ness trip again, and this time I'm determined to make it without an accident." She smiled at Joelle and Hannah and turned to Josh.

"You're welcome to join us too, Josh."

Joelle looked at her trainer with terror in her eyes. Josh couldn't come with them, not visible at least. If Josh joined them, Ruth would make them stay in the same bedroom since everyone believed that they were married. The thought alone made her blush.

Josh grinned when he saw how freaked out she was. He winked at her, gently squeezed her hand and turned to Ruth.

"Thank you, that is kind, but I'm usually busy on the weekends. Besides, you deserve a girls' weekend out I'm sure. Enjoy your time without me," he replied smiling. Joelle silently sighed.

It was getting dark, and Josh and Joelle had to leave. They left, but came right back in once they were invisible.

Ruth and Hannah were sitting on the couch talking.

"Hannah tell me, why don't you want to stay at the orphanage?"

"The first one they put me in was depressing. The people who worked there made it clear that children my age had no chance of being adopted. Then they put me into foster care, but the family that took me in only looked for someone to help with the younger children. When something went wrong, I got punished for it. It got so bad that they didn't give me food for a week and locked me in my room. They only let me out for bathroom breaks."

Ruth was shocked. That was the kind of abuse she was fighting against, and a foster family should never treat a child like that.

"After that, I ran away. I got caught, and the person promised they wouldn't tell on me but they did and took me back. Every time I ran away and got caught, people lied and took me back to an orphanage. I felt like I couldn't trust anyone anymore, so I stayed on my own. The people at the orphanage here in Edinburgh are good to the kids, but I don't want to risk ending up with a family that doesn't want me."

"It's shocking that you've had to go through that. Why did you decide to trust Jo?"

"I don't know to be honest. There's something special about her. Plus, she's proved she's there for me and won't turn me in. She's so giving and loving and full of life and humour. I couldn't help but like her right away."

Hannah smiled, grabbed one of the couch pillows and put it behind her back.

Ruth smiled as well.

"I agree. She's like a loving angel, isn't she?"

Hannah nodded.

"Hannah, I need to leave too. It's getting late, and I still need to drive home. Do you want to stay with me for a while?"

"No thank you, Ruth. I'm okay here, but I appreciate your kind offer."

Hannah didn't want to cause trouble for Ruth. It was too risky to stay with her. Someone could start asking questions, and that would lead to lying.

They hugged each other and said goodbye. Hannah closed the windows and doors and got ready for the night. She felt grateful and her heart was full.

8. Loch Ness and the Military Tattoo

Ruth's little cottage near Loch Ness looked antique and yet gorgeous at the same time. It had two bedrooms, a small kitchen, a bathroom and a gorgeous living room with shelves full of books. The grey bricks were a great contrast to the beautiful blue wooden window frames and the light yellow wooden door.

Hannah fell in love with this place right away and not only enjoyed the house but also the little garden. A brick wall surrounded the entire property. Plants and flowers grew everywhere, turning the cottage into a fairy tale house.

On Saturday morning they went for a drive around the whole loch. Ruth knew a lot about the area and Hannah was eager to learn.

"Ruth, what can you tell me about Loch Ness? It looks so gorgeous and wild - just breath-taking."

They stood on a cliff and had lunch. Ruth smiled.

"It's my favourite place in Scotland and has always been a place for me to regain my strength. I love the nature around here. It feels like untouched wilderness."

She took a deep breath and told them about the lake.

"Loch Ness is the second largest Scottish loch after Loch Lomond. Its deepest point is 230 metre, deeper than the London Tower is tall, at 189 metre. It's deeper than any other loch except Loch Morar. It has more fresh water than the lakes in England and Wales combined.[5]"

Hannah was impressed. "Wow that is deep. No wonder they say Nessie lives here. There's enough room for a monster."

Ruth smiled. "That's right."

"Have you ever seen the Loch Ness monster, Ruth?"

"No I haven't, Hannah. Stories continue to be told about sightings of the monster, but I haven't seen it. I believe something is in there though."

Hannah looked at Joelle with a frightened look.

"We'd better not go swimming then."

Joelle smiled. "Yes, that's a good idea."

They continued their journey and reached a castle. It was more ruins now than a castle, and they learned that it was called the Urughart Castle.

---

[5] https://en.wikipedia.org/wiki/Loch_Ness

Hannah, who hadn't been in school for almost a year, couldn't wait to learn more about the history of this beautiful country.

"Ruth what can you tell us about this castle?"

Again Ruth smiled. "It was one of the largest strongholds of medival Scotland in its day and remains an impressive structure although it has been mostly destroyed.[6]"

"This is so amazing. Can we check it out?"

"Yes of course." They checked out the visitor centre, and watched a short film about the history of the castle. When the film was finished, they went outside and looked at the ruins.

***

Later that afternoon it began to rain, so they returned to the cottage. Joelle and Hannah sat down in the living room. Ruth made wonderfully smelling tea, took out biscuits and then joined the other two.

"Ruth can you tell me more about the history of that castle?" Ruth took another sip of her tea, grabbed a book about the castle, and started her little history lesson.

"When was the castle built?" Hannah couldn't get enough information. Ruth smiled. She loved that Hannah was so eager to learn.

"They don't know when the castle was built, but it was somewhere around the early 13th century.[7]"

"That is super old."

[6/7] https://en.wikipedia.org/wiki/Urquhart_Castle

"It sure is. The historians know the castle was destroyed after the early Jacobite Rising of 1689.[8]"

"I love listening to you, Ruth. This is fascinating and Loch Ness is beautiful." Hannah was excited and enjoying their little trip.

Joelle smiled. She was pleased that Hannah and Ruth were both happy. She enjoyed it here and hoped things would turn out well for Hannah and Ruth.

***

When Hannah was asleep that night, Joelle made herself invisible. The past two days had kept her busy.

Since she didn't have much of a chance to talk to Josh, she was eager to have a conversation with him again. They sat down on the floor.

"This is a beautiful place. I bet the angels that get to serve here love it."

Josh smiled at her excitement.

"Yes, they do. Drumnadrochit is a small village. It's peaceful. Tourists bring a little more action, but that's about it."

"I want to stay here for the rest of my life…" she paused when she saw Josh's grin and then continued with a smile. "Well, I would if I were still alive." Joelle winked at Josh and he smiled.

"I am so glad we got to go on this trip."

---

[8] https://en.wikipedia.org/wiki/Urquhart_Castle

"Me too. By the way, why weren't you excited when Ruth asked me to join you?" Josh asked grinning. He knew what Joelle's reaction would be.

She immediately blushed and wasn't sure how to respond. Josh put his arm around her shoulders and pulled her closer.

"You are not scared of me, are you?" He looked down at her, loving the moment of her being so bashful. She was so cute when she was embarrassed.

When she didn't look up, and didn't respond, he gently lifted her chin.

"You know I am teasing you, right?" She nodded.

"…As long as we are not married for real, I wouldn't want to share a bedroom with you either," he continued saying with a big smirk on his face. Joelle looked up still red-faced.

"You are unbelievable, Josh McIntosh. Why do you enjoy it so much when I am uncomfortable and embarrassed?" She elbowed him in the stomach, but it only made him laugh.

"You are just so darling when you blush. I can't help it."

"Maybe it is time to tell everyone that we aren't married," Joelle replied as she tried her hardest to make her face return to a more normal colour.

"We can't do that, Jo. This assignment was meant for a couple. They wanted to assign a married couple at first. Peter, however, felt strongly that Hannah would respond well to you. That meant you needed a male trainer to make this work. We needed to be believable in our pretended attempt to adopt Hannah, and continue to play our part in case something goes wrong and Ruth will not adopt her. That's why Faith and Blossom were only here to protect Hannah and didn't have an actual assignment for her."

"Do you think Ruth will not adopt Hannah?"

"Honestly, it's hard to say. I think she loves Hannah and wants to deep down, but she's terrified about getting emotionally attached to someone again."

Joelle understood. Losing so many loved ones in such a short time, and not having her dream fulfilled of having children, was a tough trial and would take time to conquer. Only time would tell if she was strong enough to risk giving her heart away again.

***

Back in Edinburgh, everyone prepared for one of the largest entertainment events in the world, the Royal Edinburgh Military Tattoo. Hannah was excited to experience it for the first time. She didn't know much about it and asked Ruth for information.

"The Royal Edinburgh Military Tattoo is the most spectacular show in the world. I've heard on the news that 100 million people from all over, not just Scotland, watch it on television. Nothing, beats being there in person though. It's a brilliant performance of pipers, drummers and Highland dancers, and worth every pence.

It goes on for three weeks on the Esplanade of the Edinburgh Castle and is sold out months or even a year in advance.⁹"

"That sounds so cool and brilliant."

Hannah was amazed and couldn't wait to go. Ruth had only two tickets and invited Hannah to go with her.

She apologised to Joelle, but the military tattoo was sold out. Jo ensured her that it was fine and she liked the idea of Hannah and Ruth doing something together. Jo knew she could see it, anyway.

***

During the weeks of having the military tattoo in town, the guardian angels were busier than ever. People getting drunk and fights breaking out; as fun it was, it was also out of control. Thousands of people walked the streets of Edinburgh and when someone tripped, they got injured due to the alcohol.

It was a beautiful Saturday night when Ruth took Hannah on her first tattoo experience.

Josh and Joelle kept close to Hannah and Ruth's guardian angels. Thousands of guardian angels were around, so the humans were well protected.

Hannah saw entertainers acting like statues, painted one colour. They moved only when someone wanted to have a photograph taken with them, or when they wanted to scare children who didn't realise the statues were people and not stone.

---

⁹ https://en.wikipedia.org/wiki/Royal_Edinburgh_Military_Tattoo

They saw a unicycle rider who not only rode his unicycle on the ground, but on a rope in the air juggling burning torches. Hannah couldn't stop looking around.

She had never seen so many people walking the streets of Edinburgh.

When Ruth and Hannah reached their seats, Hannah noticed the great view they had of the amazing military bands and dance groups, and Hannah loved every second of it.

It was a perfect evening, and she was happy and grateful for the chance to be part of it. Plus the queen was there too and Hannah could see her, even though she was far away in a special VIP section. The area was well protected of course.

After the two hour show and fireworks, they followed the crowd as they left the grandstands. With the masses around, it was impossible to move quickly, and required lots of patience.

When they reached the gates to the castle grounds, they heard gun shots followed by screams. Panic arose, and the people pushed and ran.

Ruth kept Hannah close to her, but during the panic they were separated and Hannah fell to the ground, leaving little chance of not being trampled to death.

Jo threw herself on Hannah, to protect her body as much as possible, and then she touched her fingers together to stop the time.

"Josh, what are we going to do?" He turned around and the other angels came closer.

"That's a good question, Jo." He looked worried as he had never seen such a huge group stampede before, and didn't know what to do either. Jo had an idea.

"Do you think it would work if every single angel stood in front of a human and calmed them down one by one? We could even ask some angels in heaven to come down."

Josh smiled at her. "Great thinking, Jo."

They spread out and Josh called more angels from above. Once they were positioned, Jo touched her fingers together, and started the time again.

Before anyone realised what was happening, the angel force had stared everyone down and the humans came to a halt.

Everyone was surprised at the change and didn't know what to say or think. Someone picked up Hannah who had only received bruises. The police later caught the person who had caused the panic, and Ruth was so happy when she found Hannah alive.

"Wow! That was mad. I thought I would die. Why did everyone came to a halt?"

"I have no idea, Hannah. It was strange, like an invisible power or force had stopped the crowd." Ruth looked up towards heaven and said a grateful prayer.

Josh and Jo waved at Taylor, and a few other angels. The angels on earth followed their humans, and everyone was relieved that it had turned out well.

When Josh noticed the two evil angels that had caused the stampede, he waved his fist at them.

"If you dimwits ever pull something like that again, I'll punch you so hard that you'll end up in Australia." He shouted it across the street.

They only laughed at him, but he was furious.

Jo had never seen him like this before. She touched him gently on the arm. Josh looked down at her and she gave him the calming look.

"It's okay, Josh. Getting angry at those blokes will not help. They won't ever change."

"I guess you're right." He put his arm around her shoulders and they followed Hannah and Ruth to make sure Hannah was safe.

***

When they got back to the Guardian Angel Agency office that night, Sydney and Paul arrived. Paul hadn't talked to Joelle at all the past few weeks, but today he walked towards her.

"Oi Jo, great job on stopping the crowd. That was a brilliant idea. You showed those evil angels who is boss." He smiled at her and she smiled back.

Sydney stepped closer.

"Paul spotted the evil angels first. He was so angry that those stupid angels put so many human lives in danger, he attacked them right after Jo had stopped time and threw them across the castle," Sydney said. She was proud of him.

Paul smiled.

"Jo, I want to apologise to you. You were right! I was a tosser. I would still be like that if it weren't for you. I thought a lot about your words, but have been able to change some of my bad habits and will continue to do so. I never once considered your feelings, and that you have every right to say no. I only thought about myself, and that I wanted to be the one deciding how a relationship should be and work. I now understand why so many women avoided me, and why they were so upset and angry at me. Thank you for being an honest friend. It made me realise how wrong I was."

Josh's mouth dropped.

Sydney smiled since she had noticed Paul's change of heart and had seen how kind and loving he was now.

"Paul I'm so glad you're not angry at me. I never said those things to hurt you. I hope you know that? And I'm sorry too about the things I said. I was angry and upset but I should have never said that."

"Don't worry, Jo. You were right. I behaved awful, arrogant and selfish. I have to admit, at first I was offended and angry, but after a while I thought about it and recognised the truth. Thanks again."

He wanted to shake her hand, but this time she hugged him.

9. Don't Judge a Book By its Cover

The next few months flew by. Josh and Joelle were an amazing team and continued to get along well. Ruth loved Hannah, but was still hesitant to take the step of adopting her. She was scared to raise a soon-to-be teenager by herself.

As November began, Hannah ran into a girl on her way home from the fish-and-chips shop behind the park. They talked and discovered that they were the same age and didn't live far from each other.

Hannah was careful, and didn't tell Alissa that she was an orphan and didn't have a real home, but Alissa seemed to like her.

Alissa told Hannah that she had moved to Edinburgh right after the summer holidays. Her mum had passed away, and she was living with her dad and stepmother now. She was from Aberdeen and still homesick for her friends and grandparents. Since Alissa had made no friends yet, she gladly hung out with Hannah.

They met at the park every day. It was good for both girls, and they enjoyed each other's company.

Ruth was pleased when she noticed that Hannah had made a friend. It would make getting used to school so much easier for her once she went again.

Joelle and Josh were happy to see that Hannah had someone around who was her age. They liked Alissa and encouraged the two girls to play together.

After a while Hannah felt comfortable enough to tell Alissa the entire truth. Alissa was shocked. She had wondered why Hannah didn't go to school, but had been too shy to ask about it. Now she knew. She was good at keeping secrets and since she saw that Hannah was in good hands with Ruth and Joelle around; she didn't feel worried.

***

It was late in the afternoon on November 17th when Hannah and her friend Alissa were walking home from an indoor pool they had gone to together. It was cold, and snow covered the park, when two older boys spotted the girls and threw hard icy snowballs at them.

Joelle, getting furious, wanted to interfere but Josh held her back. They were invisible and couldn't do much, anyway.

"Oi, you two, leave the girls alone and get lost!" shouted a tall man at the boys from across the park.

He had been laying on a bench, but was getting up. He looked angry and scary, and the two boys ran off.

While walking towards the girls, the man stumbled and Alissa pulled Hannah's arm.

"He's probably drunk!"

Hannah looked at her friend.

"How do you know? Have you asked him?"

Confused Alissa didn't know what to say.

"No," she said. "How could I have asked him? I don't know him."

"Well, then how can you tell he's drunk?"

Alissa's face turned red.

"He looks like it," she mumbled, watching the man coming towards them.

"Are you all right?" the man asked.

"Yes thank you," Hannah said with a smile. He smiled back at her.

"Stupid lads. They always think they're so strong and powerful." He winked at Hannah and she smiled again.

"Thanks again, Mister…?"

He shook her outstretched hand.

"Henry Martin."

"Nice to meet you, Mister Martin," she said. "My name is Hannah, and this is my friend Alissa."

Alissa was not happy that Hannah talked to a stranger and shared their names with him. She tugged on Hannah's arm again to get her to leave with her. When Hannah didn't move, she stepped away a few steps and looked back at her friend with impatience.

"Please, call me Henry," he said. "It was nice to meet you too, Hannah, but now you'd better run off. It's cold out here."

Hannah nodded, gave him another warm smile, and followed her friend.

Joelle and Josh smiled at each other.

Henry Martin watched as the two girls continued their walk through the park.

"Sweet lass," Henry mumbled to himself as he walked back to his bench.

***

Joelle bit her lip while glancing around to find Henry's guardian angels. They followed him and waved at Joelle and Josh before they disappeared in the distance.

"What are you thinking, Jo?" Josh asked.

She had learned by now to control her thoughts so he couldn't read them anymore.

"I'm thinking Henry Martin would make a fine husband for Ruth and a great dad for Hannah."

Josh smiled. "You'd think something like that. Don't get your hopes up though. I'm not sure Ruth is interested or ready to meet another man. After all she loved her husband very much."

"I know, but you have to agree they would be wonderful together."

"Yes," he agreed hesitantly, "but his thoughts tell me he's not even looking for a wife."

"No matter. Thoughts can change. He hasn't met the right person yet." She grinned, and he grinned too.

"Well we're here for Hannah as her guardian angels and not as a marriage brokerage. So stick to your assignment little missy." He gave her a warning look, but Joelle smiled with the new idea fixed in her mind.

***

Alissa turned to her friend as soon as they were far enough from Henry Martin.

"Why were you so friendly to him? He's probably a drunk or homeless bloke. He could have attacked us."

She looked upset, but Hannah didn't care.

"Why wouldn't I be friendly to him? Don't you think he meets enough rude people? He helped us by scaring the boys away and didn't mean to attack us. You're judging him by his looks." She looked annoyed and Alissa frowned.

"He looks like a homeless person. And homeless people are alcoholics or on drugs," she insisted.

"Alissa let me tell you something. I don't like it when people judge other people. Its mean and cruel and you have no right to say what person he is by looking at him."

Alissa turned red again. Her whole life she had been taught not to talk to strangers. Her mum had never talked to or smiled at homeless people. Her stepmother had taught her they were just too lazy to work and instead tried to get money from other people by begging. *Why would Hannah think otherwise?*

"I was homeless for a few months. I met lots of different people and I learned that most first impressions aren't true. I lived in homeless shelters and met wonderful but sad people. Not everyone who is out begging is homeless, but they beg because they don't want to work. Often the people not begging are the ones with nothing, but still have pride in themselves and rather search for food than ask for help."

Alissa stayed quiet. She had never thought about it that way.

Hannah continued: "I've also met people that weren't as kind as they pretended to be. That's when we have to listen to what we're feeling in here," she pointed at her heart, "to see if we can trust the person. Mister Martin is a fine and kind person. There was sadness in his eyes and the little smile I gave him, and the little conversation I had with him probably made his day."

Alissa couldn't help but be impressed by her friend. She seemed so wise.

The next day, while walking to Ruth's office, Hannah ran into Henry Martin again. He walked toward the office buildings.

When Hannah recognised him, she walked faster and caught up with him.

"Hello, Henry," she said once she was next to him.

"Well hello, Hannah." He smiled at her.

She grinned back and since he looked cold, she invited him into Ruth's office. They sat together in the waiting room.

"You're sweet, Hannah, but aren't you afraid that others might laugh at you, or give you a hard time when they see you with me?"

She shook her head. "Why should I care what others think?"

Astonished he glanced at her.

"But you shouldn't be so quick to trust a stranger. After all, you don't know me."

She gave him another warm smile. "True, but I don't care. I know what you're going through."

He looked confused.

"I was homeless too, a few months ago. They sent me to an orphanage after my parents died, but I didn't want to stay there. I kept running away until I arrived here in Edinburgh and met the most amazing person ever. Her name is Joelle, and she's some sort of agent that has been taking care of me ever since we met. Joelle taught me that listening to your feelings is a good thing. She helped me trust people again."

Jo smiled when she heard Hannah praising her. Josh put his arm around her shoulders and winked at Joelle with a grin on his face.

"Is this the agent's office?" Henry asked looking around uncomfortable.

Hannah shook her head. "No, this is Ruth Smith's office. She's a lawyer and we're friends, too. We have lunch together sometimes."

Henry listened while Hannah talked away. She turned to him and asked: "What happened to you?"

A sad smile appeared on his face.

"I had a bad upbringing. Both my parents were alcoholics. I grew up with violence in the home, never enough to eat and with no love. My parents made it clear to me, and my siblings, that we weren't wanted and that they expected us to earn our own money if we wanted to stay. Eventually I turned to alcohol and drugs too," he said.

"It was my life for many years and led to losing jobs, stealing and ending up in prison. I hated myself, but couldn't get out of that cycle. One day I met a young lass who was like a guardian angel. She befriended me even though I had nothing and still got drunk regularly. But what struck me was that she never gave up on me. She never failed me as a friend. She talked me into going into rehab. When I first got there, I didn't want to be there and didn't think it would work. I was convinced nothing would change, and that I wasn't strong enough to turn things around. I wanted to give up and go back to my old, bad life. Then she said something I will never forget: *'Giving up is for losers, Henry. You are a son of God and shouldn't treat yourself like this. He loves you and it's time now to love yourself and treat yourself with the respect you truly deserve.'"*

Ruth stood at the door, listening to the conversation. She was touched by what he said, but seeing a homeless person in her office was not something she was comfortable with.

Hannah smiled at Henry.

"Do you remember the girl's name?"

"I do. I will never forget it. She too worked for some sort of agency. Her name was Taylor."

***

Joelle looked up at Josh. "Taylor? The same Taylor that took care of me when I died and brought me to Scotland?"

Josh nodded and Joelle smiled.

"That sure sounds like her. She was direct and straight forward with me, too."

***

At that moment, Hannah noticed Ruth and jumped up.

"Ruth," she said, "this is Henry Martin."

He stood up too. "I shouldn't be here, anyway. Thanks for getting me out of the cold."

Ruth nodded, not saying a word.

"Maybe you could shovel snow every morning to earn money?" Hannah looked at Ruth who didn't know what to say.

He glanced at Ruth and figured she wouldn't want that, anyway.

"It's okay, Hannah, I'll be okay."

"Do you have a job, Henry?"

"No." He had to admit.

"Why not?"

"I've tried several times. I never make it past the job interview. The interview is over as soon as people find out I've been to prison. Nobody wants to give me a chance."

Hannah gave Ruth a pleading look to say something. She gave in.

"Mister Martin, it would be nice indeed if you could shovel snow in front of my office. It's hard work for me alone and I will pay you."

Henry looked from one to the other, nodded and left the building.

***

"Hannah, you can't invite people we don't know to come work for me. We know nothing about him. You can't be that trusting," Ruth said, looking at Hannah annoyed.

"I feel good about him, Ruth. He's a good bloke and needs help."

Ruth shook her head and turned around to go back to work.

***

Every morning before Ruth got to work, Henry had shovelled the snow and was gone before she arrived.

Other people in the offices nearby asked if he could shovel for them as well. Soon Henry was earning a decent amount of money and all because of Hannah.

Hannah was pleased, but Ruth didn't feel good about it.

***

"Ruth, why aren't you happy?" Joelle looked at her with a confused look on her face.

"Henry Martin comes more often, but I don't trust him. He's sneaking into Hannah's heart and I don't want her to get hurt."

"Hannah is good at reading people. Don't forget she has been on her own for a while."

"That's true, but we know nothing about him. He probably takes the money he earns and buys alcohol to get drunk." Joelle shot her a look.

"Do you seriously think that, Ruth?"

Josh being invisible, put his hands on Joelle's shoulders to let her know she needed to be careful and not be too pushy.

"Again, we know nothing about him."

"I think he's a kind man who had a hard life and is trying to make it right." Joelle gave Ruth a determined and stern look.

"He probably made up his story."

"Is that what you tell yourself? From what Hannah told me, he sounds like he's honest and open. Why would he lie about having an alcohol and drug problem in the past, if it wasn't true?"

Ruth looked uncomfortable.

"Maybe he said that so we would feel sorry for him."

Joelle shook her head. "I doubt that. Why would he make up a story when he knows people won't give him a chance because of it?"

***

Ruth couldn't sleep well that night. Joelle was right, and she felt guilty for feeling the way she did. But she couldn't bring herself to trust him.

***

When Henry came the next day to pick up his money, Hannah invited him inside. He was shivering and couldn't stop when he walked in.

"It's freezing in here," he said.

Ruth walked in and nodded.

"Yes, our central heating boiler broke last night and I have to get someone to come fix it."

He looked at her. "I can do it for you."

Ruth raised her eyebrow. "You know how to do that?"

"Yes, I'm good at fixing things. I've tried getting a job as a handyman, but with no success."

Again she raised an eyebrow.

"Sure, if you think you can do it. Try it."

An hour later, the heat was working again.

Impressed, Ruth paid and thanked him. Hannah smiled at both.

"Henry, you should open your own business."

"I've tried, but because of my past, the banks won't loan me any money," he said. "Thanks Ms. Smith and please let me know if anything else needs fixing around here. I'm happy to help."

As soon as he had left, Hannah turned to Ruth.

"We should help him start his own business," she said excitedly and her eyes sparkled.

"Hannah, I will not give him money. What if he takes it and runs off? It's one thing to have him do little jobs around here, but it's a different story to offer someone enough money to start their own business."

Hannah frowned. "You don't trust him, do you? Why do you keep judging him like that? He's kept his word ever since I met him. He has been shovelling snow every morning for the past two weeks. He fixed the heater, and you don't want to give him a chance?"

"I can't take the risk, Hannah." Turning around, she started to leave the room.

"I feel good about him. I feel it in here," Hannah said as she pointed to her heart. "He has been honest with us this whole time. He is doing his best to turn his life around, but still nobody will help him. I know he's a good person."

Ruth thought about Hannah's words for days.

Am I wrong?

She didn't want to trust someone only to find out later that they had used her.

What am I supposed to do?

10. Who is Joseph Walker?

A fine-looking gentleman had come into Ruth's office. At first he asked for information about child abuse, the signs of child abuse, and when it was time to report abuse. After a while he brought her flowers and lunch, and then he took her out to lunch. His name was Joseph Walker and Jo didn't feel good about him. There was something about him she didn't like.

When he first met Hannah he was friendly and polite, but his thoughts weren't kind. He didn't want to share Ruth with anyone and didn't appreciate Ruth's kind feelings towards the child.

Ruth liked Joseph a great deal. He was the first man, since her husband's death, that showed interest in her and she was open for a new relationship.

When Joelle tried to mention that she didn't know much about him, and Ruth needed to be careful, Ruth got upset.

Joelle decided to just keep an eye on him for now.

***

The first time Henry Martin ran into Joseph Walker was uncomfortable for everyone.

Henry was in the process of entering Ruth's office when Joseph, who had parked his expensive car in front of the office, stepped in front of him.

"This isn't a facility for beggars. Go away and try somewhere else." Joseph gave Henry an evil and disgusted look.

Hannah, who had appeared behind the two men, had heard the entire conversation. Henry's presence was the only thing that stopped her from giving Joseph a piece of her mind.

Joelle too was ready to snap, and it took Josh's strength to keep her from doing something she would regret later on.

"Mister Martin is doing jobs for Ruth, and so there is no need to send him away, MR. WALKER!" Hannah snapped, pronouncing his last name with emphasis. She wanted to show Joseph how displeased she was with his arrogant behaviour.

Before Joseph could respond, she turned to Henry, shook his hand and invited him inside with a smile on her face.

Joseph stepped back biting his tongue and followed the other two.

***

When Ruth walked into the waiting room and noticed Joseph, her eyes lit up right away. She greeted him enthusiastically and then saw Henry. Ashamed to see him there, she nodded coldly and paid him what she owed him.

"Thanks, Mrs. Smith."

"You're welcome. Oh and Mister Martin, your services are no longer needed." She tried to smile, but again it looked heartless which made Joelle's heart cringe. She had never seen Ruth like this.

Henry nodded, understanding perfectly, but Hannah seemed confused.

"What do you mean by his services are no longer needed?"

Ruth looked uncomfortable and turned red.

"Well the snow is gone now and nothing else needs fixing."

"But winter has just begun, it could snow any day again." Hannah looked at Ruth and she was not pleased that Ruth treated Henry this way.

Before things escalated, Henry cleared his throat.

"It's okay, Hannah. Thank you, Mrs. Smith, for letting me earn money. It's truly appreciated. I hope all goes well for you. Happy Christmas and a Happy New

Year." He nodded in Joseph and Ruth's direction and left the office.

Hannah followed him.

After Henry and Hannah had left, Ruth turned to Joseph and apologised to him for the incident. Joseph assured her it was no big deal and that he admired her kind heart.

Ruth, however, felt bad inside. The way she had treated Henry was not kind, and nothing to be proud of.

***

"Henry wait!" Hannah caught up to him and grabbed his arm. "Please don't go. I'm sorry Ruth treated you that way, but I'm sure she didn't mean to. She's been acting strange ever since that Mr. Walker came into her office." Hannah looked upset and angry while saying it.

Henry smiled at her but his eyes looked sad and tired.

"It's okay, Hannah. I'll be fine. Mrs. Smith is a wonderful woman and the fact she gave me jobs means a lot."

"No Henry, don't walk away. I'm sure if I talk to Ruth…."

"Thanks Hannah, but that wouldn't be a good idea. She seems to like Mr. Walker and having me around would make her uncomfortable. I'm a homeless person after all."

"But nobody should be uncomfortable around you."

"You're a sweet lass, Hannah. But I'm afraid most people don't feel the same way you do and that's okay. I don't even blame them. Don't be angry with Mrs. Smith. She means well."

He smiled at Hannah and went to shake her hand, but she jumped up and gave him a big hug. He was touched and cleared his throat a few times, even after the tears had stopped coming.

Hannah stepped back and looked up at him.

"Happy Christmas, Henry."

"Happy Christmas, Hannah." He kissed her head and walked off towards the park.

***

Ruth began to spent more time with Joseph Walker. They now dated, and it was only the first week of December.

Ruth also spent a lot of time with Hannah, teaching her relevant material from school so she wouldn't be so behind when she started again.

Hannah loved the time with Ruth. She was a vivacious teacher and made it fun.

***

One evening when Ruth came to the cottage to teach Hannah, Joseph was with her. Hannah had tried her best to give Joseph a fair shot, but she realised he was dishonest and superficial. His attitude showed that he didn't like her, and it made it hard for her to stay polite.

The way he had treated Henry was still vivid in her mind and she didn't want Joseph near her anymore.

Hannah couldn't understand how Ruth could even fall for this man. It was written all over his face that something was wrong with him and that he wasn't as kind and honest as he claimed to be.

Why didn't Ruth see that?

Joseph kept staring at Hannah while Ruth tried to teach her math, and it made Hannah irritable and uncomfortable.

Josh and Joelle, both invisible, felt the hatred between Joseph and the child. Jo calmed down Hannah so things wouldn't escalate.

Even though Hannah was calm now, she kept making mistakes, and it threw off Ruth.

"Hannah, you need to concentrate."

"I can't when there are other people in the room." Hannah glanced at Joseph who gave her an evil look.

"You have to be able to concentrate when the class is full of other students."

"Yes but they are my age, not adults." The twelve-year-old sat back in her chair and refused to work anymore.

Ruth sighed and gave up. She and Joseph left Hannah and went out to supper.

Joelle and Josh, wanting to know what was going on, followed them.

"Ruth, why are you teaching Hannah? She should be in school."

"Hannah lost both her parents, Joseph, and if she goes back to school, they'll put her in the orphanage again. She doesn't want to be there."

"You're a lawyer, Ruth and by hiding her you're breaking the law."

"I'm not hiding her, just haven't reported her."

"That's the same thing."

"Look Joseph, this is my decision so please stay out of it." She felt uncomfortable and even guilty, as she knew well what she ought to do, but her heart told her she did the right thing by not reporting Hannah.

Joseph said nothing anymore, but he wasn't happy that she had told him off and asked him to not interfere.

***

"Josh, he will do something to Hannah. We have to stop him."

"We don't even know what he will do, but we can keep an eye on him. I'm sure the other angels will too."

"And where are his guardian angels? I haven't seen them so far." Joelle couldn't understand that they had seen nothing of them.

"I'm guessing that they are staying at a distance. If he has evil tendencies, he will have evil angels around him and that makes his guardian angels stay away or keep their distance."

"But shouldn't he have evil angels around him?"

"Not if they are trying to make us believe he is harmless. They won't show themselves unless they want to interfere and attack us."

"Does that happen to everyone who is influenced by evil?"

He nodded.

"In the beginning we guardian angels try to influence humans for the better, but if they listen to the evil side, we have to draw ourselves back. We can't force a person to be good."

"So it's like when the little girl died because her father beat her?"

"Yes!"

"I can't read his mind either. What's up with that?" Joelle was confused. Josh looked at her.

"That's another sign he's influenced by evil angels. If they want to make sure he can do what they want him to do, they put a cloud or fog in his mind so we can't see his thoughts anymore."

"But doesn't that make him dangerous?" Joelle looked worried.

Josh nodded now.

"It does. We have to watch Hannah and Ruth closely now. I'll inform the other guardian angels as well."

***

One afternoon, while Hannah walked to the shop to get a few things, she noticed Joseph ahead of her. He

163

wasn't alone. He had a woman by his side and it wasn't Ruth.

Hannah's feelings weren't wrong after all. She followed him.

Joseph and the woman were obviously close. He kept kissing her, and had his arm around her waist.

Josh and Joelle also followed. It looked like they would finally get answers.

Joseph and his woman friend, reached a block of flats. While the woman unlocked the door to the building, he noticed Hannah who stood behind a car. Anger built quickly, and he had to calm himself to speak politely to his female friend.

"Sweetheart, I want to get something out of my car and will be right up."

She nodded and walked inside.

He pretended to walk to his car, grabbed Hannah by her jacket and pulled her with him into an alley right next to the building.

He pushed the child against the wall.

"What are you doing here?"

She gave him an angry look. "I followed you because I don't trust you. Now I know for sure you're a liar. I'm sure Ruth will be delighted to hear the truth about you."

He squeezed her arms so hard, it began to hurt.

"Let me tell you something you little beast, if you tell anything to Ruth, I'll get rid of you and make sure that nobody knows where you are or what's happened to you. Ruth believes me and I'll make sure she thinks you're the liar and not me."

Hannah tried to get away from him, but he held her tight.

"We'll see if she believes you more than me. You're a tosser Joseph Walker!"

Furious he lifted his hand to slap her across the face.

"DON'T YOU DARE STRIKE THAT CHILD!" shouted Joelle as she stepped into the alley from behind the building. She pulled him backwards and away from Hannah.

Joseph was startled and winced when he heard Joelle's voice, and felt her firm grip on his arm. He stepped back. It not only surprised him that this woman had appeared, but he wondered if she had heard the whole conversation. That made it much more complicated because she clearly knew Hannah.

"Can you explain why you had her pushed against the wall, and were about to hit her?" Joelle asked furious.

Her eyes were as cold as ice and Josh stepped behind her now, putting his hands on her shoulders so she calmed down again. She was ready to rip Joseph's head off.

"She took something, and I wanted it back."

"And because she didn't give it back, you were going to beat it out of her?"

"She was disrespectful and rude!"

165

"That is no excuse! You have no right to strike that child."

"What's it to you? You have nothing to do with this," he snapped, but kept away from her.

"I will let no one lay hands on a weaker person if I am around and can do something about it. You don't just take matters into your own hands! What do we have the police force for?"

He looked at her not knowing what to say.

"If Hannah took something we should call the police because stealing is something that needs to be punished."

Hannah heard the sarcasm in Joelle's voice and grinned.

Joseph became uncomfortable. The last thing he wanted was the police. Hannah had seen the woman by his side and if the police came, they would question everything. Hannah would mention his female friend and everything came out.

"No it's okay. She stole nothing. It was just a big misunderstanding. It wasn't that important and I am sure Hannah learned her lesson, right Hannah?" Joseph swallowed, trying to be cool and forgiving.

Hannah looked at him furious, but before she could say anything someone else stepped into the alley.

"Henry!" Hannah hadn't seen him in a while and jumped into his arms. He smiled at her, but gave Joseph a furious and aggressive look.

He had seen Hannah following Joseph, and a feeling told him to follow them too to make sure she was safe. Henry was grateful that he had listened to his instincts.

Joseph couldn't believe what was happening. Where did these two come from? He saw Joelle grinning, and Henry staring at him, and it made him become angrier and angrier.

"What are you doing here dosser? Out begging again? Not smart enough to work or have a home, eh?" Joseph grinned a nasty grin at the other man.

Henry continued to stare at him. Henry's guardian angels calmed down Henry so things wouldn't escalate. The tension between the two men was intense.

"… say's the person with such a wee brain." Joelle mumbled the words more to herself, but Henry, Josh and Henry's guardian angels had to hide their smiles when they heard it.

Hannah had not heard it and she was furious.

"Dosser? How dare you talk to Henry that way, MR. WALKER! YOU aren't even good enough to tie his shoes for him. YOU are a true foul git and…"

"Come Hannah let's walk home." Henry turned to Hannah, took her by the hand and pulled her out of the alley. He didn't want things to escalate. Hannah wasn't scared and wanted to say more rude things to Joseph.

Joseph had to force himself to control his temper because he was ready to snap.

Once Henry and Hannah were out of earshot, Joelle came within inches of Joseph's face.

"Listen, Joseph Walker. If you ever try to hurt Hannah, or ever threaten her like that again, you will have to answer to me."

He laughed uncomfortably. "Oh am I supposed to feel threatened now?"

She grinned. "No that's not a threat, that's a promise." She turned around and walked away following Henry and Hannah.

Joseph felt intimidated and scared. He didn't understand why he felt that way since she was a woman, and much smaller than him. He shook it off and tried to calm himself.

Once he was relaxed enough, he took out his mobile phone and called Ruth to tell her the story and make sure she heard it from him first.

As soon as Joelle had walked out of the alley, Josh erased the encounter with Joelle from Joseph's memory so he wouldn't remember her if they met again. He had a terrible feeling about him and would definitely keep an eye on him.

***

"Hannah, never follow that man again. You were lucky that Mr. Martin, and I were around. Joseph is dangerous and you can't trust him." Joelle gave her a serious look and Henry nodded.

"I don't trust him. He threatened me, but he lies to Ruth. I can't let that happen."

"You need to stay away from him."

Hannah nodded and smiled at Henry again.

"Thank you so much for helping me."

"No problem. I did nothing, this lass here seemed in control of the situation. If anything I made it worse with my appearance." He looked into Joelle's eyes and smiled.

Hannah, who realised that Joelle and Henry hadn't met yet, stepped next to Joelle.

"Oh Henry, this is Joelle. You know the agent I talked about."

Henry nodded with a grin. "That's her, I see." He looked her up and down. "I thought so already."

Joelle blushed but grinned too.

"I've heard about you as well, Mr. Martin."

"Oh, please call me Henry."

"My pleasure. I'm Jo." She shook his hand, and they walked through the park together. Henry escorted them to the cottage and only then did he turn around to walk back to the homeless shelter.

***

When Hannah entered her cottage, she called Ruth.

"Ruth I saw Joseph today, and he has been lying to you this whole time. He has another girlfriend."

Ruth laughed. "Oh Hannah don't worry. Joseph called me and told me everything. He told me you saw him with his sister and that you might think she's his girlfriend."

"That wasn't his sister, Ruth, he kissed her and…"

"Yes he told me it must have looked like they kissed when he hugged her goodbye."

"That's not true, Ruth. He is lying…"

"Stop, Hannah. You're getting yourself worked up over something that isn't even true. Drop it okay?" She hung up.

"What happened?" Joelle asked, giving Hannah a puzzled look.

"She hung up on me. Joseph called her and told her that the woman he was with was his sister." Hannah was so shocked that Ruth hadn't believed her she had to sit down.

***

During the next few days, Hannah had to put up with Joseph. She tried avoiding him as much as possible, but Ruth kept bringing him by, hoping they would get along.

***

At the night of the 3rd Advent they had supper together at the cottage. Joelle was there as well.

Ruth introduced Joelle and Joseph and went into the kitchen to prepare the food. Hannah followed Ruth to help her with the preparations.

Joseph watched Joelle. She did not like the look he gave her. It made her uncomfortable and suspicious.

"So," he said, as he got up and sat himself right next to Joelle, "Ruth told me you are an agent. Are you in the police force?"

"No!"

"No? Are you from the Security Service, FBI or CIA? I can't imagine considering you are such a young pretty little thing." He moved closer and stroked her leg with two of his fingers.

At that point she really wanted to put him in his place, but she also wanted to know how far he would go. She pretended to be insecure and shy.

"I am not an FBI, Security Service or CIA agent."

"What agency do you belong to, then?"

"I can't tell you that." She glanced over her shoulder towards the kitchen, making it seem like she was waiting for Ruth to return.

"You can tell me, Joelle. I promise I won't tell anyone," he said with a nasty smile on his face.

Before Jo knew what was happening, he had his arm around her shoulders.

"Are you trying to hit on me? Please don't do that." She tried to get out of his embrace, but he only put his arm around her waist and pulled her closer.

"Why? Shouldn't you be able to defend yourself, as an agent?"

"Let go of me!" She tried to push him away from her, but he obviously enjoyed being in charge, and put his other hand on her knee now.

When he moved his hand up and down her leg, she pushed him away from her and jumped up.

"I have asked you to stop touching me and that does not mean you can continue. I don't appreciate your sexual advances, and I am sure Ruth would not be happy if she found out you touch other women inappropriately." Joelle was furious, but she knew she had to play her part well if she wanted to look behind his evil facade.

Joseph stood up and stepped closer again. He obviously wasn't someone who took no for an answer because he stroked her upper arm now.

"How would Ruth find out?"

"I could tell her."

"And what good would that do? Guess whom she believes before anyone else? Me! So I recommend you keep your cute little mouth shut!"

He was about to grab Joelle's face to kiss her lips, when he heard Hannah come in. With one quick movement he turned around and sat back on his chair, like he was Mr. Innocent himself.

***

Joelle couldn't believe what had happened. She looked at Josh and Ruth's guardian angels, and they were as stunned as she was. He had barely met her and hit on her so aggressively?

What a disgusting man! I can't believe he would do something like that, with Ruth being right there. I mean how many women does one man need?

"He is a pervert for sure. I wonder why he thinks he can get away with this. What else is that dirt bag hiding?" Josh was angry and shocked that Joseph invaded someone's personal space in such a disturbing way.

Joelle stayed away from Joseph the rest of the night. It made him feel powerful, and he gave her a smudgy smile every so often because he knew she couldn't tell on him without ruining her friendship with Ruth.

Jo was beyond disgusted.

After supper they sat back in the living room, and Ruth beamed at Joelle and Hannah.

"I have an announcement to make," she said. "Joseph proposed last night and we're getting married." Her eyes sparkled, and she lovingly hugged her now fiancé.

Joelle and Hannah exchanged a quick glance, both in shock. Joelle found her voice first and congratulated them, but she was not happy about it. She only gave them the obligatory congratulations.

Hannah said nothing for a long time. She then got up and hugged Ruth, wishing her the best. Everyone in the room noticed how she ignored Joseph and pretended he didn't exist.

Ruth looked worried and uncomfortable, and Joseph could barely control his temper, but decided not to say anything.

After Joseph had left that night, Ruth confronted Hannah and Joelle.

"Can you two tell me why you were so rude to that man?" Her eyes were angry, but Joelle noticed worry in her voice.

Before Jo could respond, Hannah snapped.

"I will not pretend I'm happy for you, Ruth. He hates me and I've tried to tell you what kind of person he is, but you won't…"

"Do you believe that too, Jo?" Ruth interrupted, looking now at Joelle.

"Ruth…"

"Fine, hate him. Think whatever you want. I'm not asking you to like the man, but I love him. I don't understand why you so desperately try to spread lies, Hannah, but for your information it won't change my mind. I like both of you, and I want us to get along, so please at least try to accept him the way he is. I had planned on spending Christmas with you, Hannah, but the way things are now, I don't think it would be a good idea. Happy Christmas." She looked at them unhappy and left the house.

Joelle and Hannah stood there for a few minutes not sure what to say or think. After a while Hannah turned around and looked at her guardian angel.

"Can you believe this, Jo? How can she accept his proposal? Why can't she see he's dishonest?" Hannah was shocked beyond imagination. She had accepted that Ruth brought him around for visits, and dealt with it hoping that they would break up on their own, but this sudden engagement changed everything.

Joelle didn't respond right away. She hadn't seen this coming and was disturbed by the news. She looked at Josh trying to get guidance and comfort from him, but he was as baffled as everyone else and shrugged his shoulders.

"I wish I could give you an answer, Hannah. I don't know why she can't see it, but we can only hope and pray that with time she'll see what's happening. Until then we have to do our best to be kind and not make matters worse."

***

When Jo and Josh went back to the agency that night, they walked home through the park. Josh was invisible, but Joelle wasn't. It was dark, but the moon lit up their way.

They hadn't gone far when a man hurried towards Joelle. It was Joseph Walker.

"What are you doing here, Mr. Walker?" Joelle gave him an angry look.

"I waited for you so we could talk more. I figured it would be best not to talk in Ruth's presence." He stepped in her way and grabbed her hands.

"It was wise not to say anything, Joelle, because as you can see, Ruth is in love with me."

"I wonder if she would still be in love with you if she knew what for a disgusting dirt bag you are!" She tried to get away from him, but he pulled her closer.

"And yet she will never find out!" He grabbed both her wrists with one hand and used his other hand to touch her face. She tried to get away from him, but he was strong, and Jo didn't want to use her angel strength yet. When he kissed her neck, she kicked him against his chin and pushed him away from her.

"She will find out if you don't stay away from me. I have told you several times now to stop touching me. I don't want to be touched by you, and I am disgusted by you and your lies. What you did, and are doing right now, is sexual harassment and I could report you for it."

He was shocked how confident Joelle was suddenly.

"But you won't do that because Ruth won't believe you!"

"Ruth might not, but the police will!" She looked at him with a firm expression and that made him angry.

He grabbed her by her arms.

"Are you threatening me you little witch? I can show you what real sexual harassment is!"

Joelle removed his hands from her arms, pushed him away from her and stepped backwards. When she tried to walk past him, he grabbed her around her waist and pulled her backwards, off the path.

She stepped on his foot and slammed her elbow into his rips.

"I would leave now if I were you! If not, you will end up in prison tonight," she said when she was free.

That moment, as if on cue, Josh and three more male angels made themselves visible and stepped from behind the trees on to the path. Joseph was shocked. He had expected no witnesses.

"Never underestimate the power of agents, no matter what type of agents they are!" Joelle's look meant business and Joseph turned around and disappeared without saying another word.

When Joseph was gone, Joelle breathed through her teeth. She was shaking with anger and frustration, and tears entered her eyes.

Despite her being an angel, and trying to appear tough and strong, being targeted like that was traumatising. She hated that there were guys out there who forced themselves on women, no matter what.

She was creeped out and felt awful for women who were true victims of sexual harassment or even worse, assault.

Josh lovingly pulled Joelle into his arms and held her until she calmed down again. It made him angry that Joseph victimised women and treated them with so little respect.

After Jo had her emotions in check, the angels made themselves invisible.

"Now we need to find out what else he is hiding. He targets women, to sexually harass them, but I think he has more secrets than that," Josh said as he put his arm around Joelle's shoulder.

11. What Are We Going to Do?

Since Ruth and Joseph weren't coming for Christmas Eve, Hannah invited Henry instead. He was lonely and could use a nice warm meal. Joelle and Josh were coming too and they could keep each other company.

Early in the morning on Christmas Eve, Hannah went out to find Henry. She found him on a bench near the loch.

He was surprised to see her.

"Hannah, what are you doing here this early in the morning?"

"I was looking for you and wanted to invite you for supper tonight!"

"I don't think Mrs. Smith would be okay with that, Hannah." Henry was touched that this sweet child reached out to him, but he knew Ruth wouldn't approve.

"She won't be there. She got engaged to Joseph a week ago and wants to celebrate with him alone since Jo and I aren't too fond of him," Hannah responded, rolling her eyes.

Henry turned pale for a moment, but gained control right away.

***

"Did you see that, Josh?" Joelle looked at her trainer, who nodded. They were both invisible and saw the reaction on his face. "He's in love with Ruth."

"Now don't jump to conclusions, Jo." Josh glanced at her, but she had already read Henry's thoughts.

His guardian angels smiled when they saw Joelle grinning from ear to ear.

"He loves her."

"Listen Jo, even if Henry loves her it doesn't change that Ruth is engaged to Joseph."

"True, but we have to prove to Ruth that Henry is the better man." She grinned again.

***

"Hannah I'm not sure that's a good idea. Mrs. Smith made it clear that she doesn't want me around."

"But I do. Please Henry. It means so much to me."

"Mrs. Smith is your foster mum, I can't go against her wishes."

Hannah looked surprised. She had forgotten that he didn't know she lived by herself.

"No, Ruth isn't my foster mum."

She told him everything, and he went from being in shock to feeling grateful that he had followed his instinct of watching Hannah the day she spied on Joseph.

"Well in that case, I'd love to join you, Hannah."

***

It was a pleasant and enjoyable evening. They ate delicious food, read the nativity story together and played games. They were sitting together in the living room with hot chocolate and the fire place burning, when Ruth walked in.

"Happy Christmas Han…" Startled she looked from Joelle to Hannah to Henry. "What are you doing here, Mr. Martin?" Her demeanour became distant and reserved, but before Henry could say anything, Hannah stood up.

"I invited him over. You can join us too. We have hot chocolate left." She smiled at Ruth, but Ruth shook her head.

"No, thank you. I've only come by to say Happy Christmas." She smiled at everyone and then looked at Joelle.

"Jo, may I speak to you for a moment?"

"Sure." Joelle stood up and followed Ruth out of the room.

***

"How can you let Hannah invite that man? How can you let her tell him where she lives?"

Joelle raised an eyebrow. "Why wouldn't I?"

"Why wouldn't you? He's a stranger and we know nothing about him. She gave him access and permission to come back and steal whenever he wants. He might hurt her."

Joelle tried to bite her tongue, but her sense for fairness took over and she snapped.

"You let Joseph come here, don't you?"

"That's different."

"How so? He's a stranger too and we know nothing about him."

"You are being judgmental, Joelle. Joseph is a fine man and I love him. He has my full trust."

"I'm being judgmental? What about you and your accusations and thoughts about Henry? He has done nothing wrong and deserves to be treated with dignity and respect. He adores Hannah and would never hurt her."

"Still, he shouldn't have come here knowing I'm not okay with it." Ruth felt ashamed of herself because she knew well that Joelle was right even though she would not admit it.

"That's what Henry told Hannah when she first invited him. He told her he shouldn't be here because you wouldn't want that."

"Really?"

"Yes. But Hannah insisted. You know how she is." Joelle smiled, trying to calm Ruth and herself down, and it worked.

Ruth smiled too. "That's true. Well enjoy the rest of the evening, Jo. Happy Christmas."

"Happy Christmas to you, too."

When Joelle returned to the living room, Henry stood up.

"I should leave now. I knew it wasn't a good idea to come here."

"It's okay, Henry. Ruth was just surprised to see you here. She isn't trying to interfere and delighted that we're together on this special night." She smiled a winning smile at him and he grinned.

"Really?"

"Yes, cross my heart."

***

Ruth, Joseph and Hannah had supper again a few days later. Ruth wanted to give it another try. To her surprise Hannah stayed polite, even to Joseph… at first.

He, however, was still upset and angry at Hannah and how she had treated him after they had announced their engagement. He was determined to destroy Hannah's relationship with Ruth.

Joseph left the room for a moment, and when he came back accused Hannah of having taken money out of his wallet.

Hannah stood up furious. "How dare you accuse me of something like that? Maybe it's your old age, and you forgot where you put it."

He got up and wanted to slap her, but Ruth stood between them and stopped him.

Hannah had not moved an inch and showed him she did not fear him.

Joseph pretended to be offended and left straight away. It wasn't until after he left that Ruth turned around angry.

"Hannah, you need to be more respectful. Your behaviour today was rude and I want you to apologise tomorrow."

"I will not apologise, Ruth. He accused me of stealing money. Why would I steal anyone's money?"

"You don't like him. Maybe you're trying to get him into trouble?" Ruth sat down on the couch in the spot Hannah had been sitting earlier and while moving the pillow she felt something. She reached underneath and found a five pound bill. "And what is this?"

Hannah shook her head.

"He put it there to make you believe I stole the money."

"That's ridiculous. I expect of you to return the money tomorrow and apologise."

"I will not do that. He's a filthy liar."

"HANNAH!" Ruth was furious now.

"You don't believe me, do you? You're on his side, even though you've known me much longer."

"He's an adult and you need to treat him with respect."

"I respect adults as long as they don't lie about me. I never took that money. Yes, I don't like him, and you know why, but that's not my problem. How about you focus on him not liking me either? He too has a reason to play these stupid games and get me into trouble." Her look was stern and direct. There was no false dignity in her voice.

Ruth didn't see that. She gave Hannah a disappointed look and left.

***

"She totally believes that git, Josh. We have to stop her before she does something stupid."

"We can't, Jo. It's her choice and if she wants to take his word over Hannah's, and turn against her, there's nothing we can do."

"But she's perfect for Hannah and if she marries Joseph, Ruth will never adopt her."

Joelle was angry and frustrated. She saw the injured look on Hannah's face and knew Joseph had already damaged the trust Hannah had in Ruth.

The next morning, when Ruth saw Joseph, she returned the money and apologised for Hannah. He showed her a long scratch on his car, accusing Hannah again. It hurt Ruth that Hannah would do something like that.

***

After the incidents, Ruth pulled back from Joelle and Hannah. She didn't like the tension between Hannah and

Joseph, and since he was now part of her life, she only saw the girl every few days.

***

A few days after the incident with the money, Joelle decided to have a serious talk with Ruth. Maybe if she told Ruth about Joseph's behaviour towards her, things would change. It was a risk to take, but Joelle didn't know what else to do.

When she entered Ruth's office, Ruth greeted her with a smile, but unfortunately Joseph was there as well.

"I am glad you are here, Jo, because I have something to tell you. Joseph, would you mind waiting outside?" He shook his head, lovingly squeezed Ruth's arm and left the room.

Before Joelle could even say anything, Ruth spoke again.

"I have decided not to adopt Hannah. We are not a good match. It's not working out." She didn't look happy sharing these news, but Joelle was so in shock, she didn't even see that.

"What?"

"I am sorry, Jo, but with Joseph in my life now, and Hannah not getting along with him, it wouldn't be wise to adopt her. Please find someone else."

"But, Ruth…" Joelle began before Ruth interrupted her.

"My mind is made up. Hannah can stay at the cottage until you have found someone else. In the meantime please continue to look after her because I will cut my visits to a minimum."

As soon as Joelle left the building, she made herself invisible and broke out in tears. Josh pulled her lovingly into his arms, but he was shocked himself. They both knew Joseph had caused problems, but they did not expect Ruth to pull back completely.

It took Jo a while until she calmed down again. She was heartbroken and didn't know how to solve this problem. How could they make Ruth see what an evil person Joseph Walker was?

***

"Why does Ruth spend so much time with that bloke? Can't she see that something is wrong with him?"

Joelle and Hannah sat together on the couch in the cottage and relaxed together. Hannah hadn't seen Ruth in a while and missed her motherly friend.

Joelle hadn't told Hannah about Ruth's decision because she couldn't make herself do it, nor did she want to make matters worse.

"I have no idea, Hannah. She likes him. Maybe he's not as bad as we think," she said, even though she didn't believe it herself. Sometimes it was best not to stir the pot.

"You know what's wrong with him. You and Henry heard how he threatened me after I saw him with his girlfriend."

Joelle nodded.

"He also accused me of stealing money."

Hannah hadn't told Joelle about the money incident. Joelle acted surprised and shocked.

"What?"

"Yes, and Ruth found the money behind a pillow. She wanted me to apologise for something I didn't even do. One day later, she blamed me again saying I scratched Joseph's car. She doesn't believe me."

"That's shocking, Hannah. I'm sorry to hear it."

"Doesn't matter now. He got what he wanted. She doesn't spend time with me anymore and is convinced he is right and honest, and I am the liar. I was hoping Ruth would adopt me. I thought she loved and cared about me, but with this man in the picture I doubt that will happen. I'm waiting for them to report me to the orphanage, or kick me out of this cottage since this is Ruth's place now, not mine."

It broke Joelle's heart to see Hannah so sad and disappointed. But she didn't know what to do.

"Do you want me to talk to, Ruth?"

"It will not make a difference. She'll think you're against Joseph too and that you're trying to bad-mouth him. It's like she's blind or something and can't see how he's trying so hard to split us up."

***

Ruth, who stood in front of the open window of the living room, had heard every word. *Was Joseph trying to get rid of Hannah?* He had been successful at keeping her occupied and not leaving any free time this week. It made her think.

Have I been unfair to Hannah? She was always honest with me before. Why would she lie now? Plus Joseph keeps bringing up Hannah even though we're not around her, and I made the decision of not adopting her. Is he trying to split us up? Had he been deceiving her even though she had been so sure of his character?

Something was wrong, and Ruth had to claim her life back. She had to make it clear to Joseph that she would continue to see Hannah, whether or not he liked it.

She had planned on visiting Hannah that night to have a New Year's Eve celebration, but figured it was best to let everyone cool down. Instead she went back home and called Joseph. She informed him that she would cancel the next night's supper plans and spend the evening with Hannah instead. She told him she would spend more time with Hannah again and that she expected him to respect that.

He was furious when he received her call. He thought he had been successful in keeping Ruth and Hannah apart, but clearly it wasn't enough. Joseph knew if Ruth and Hannah spent time together, Ruth would believe her and might even change her mind about the adoption. He didn't like children and he would not sit back and watch this orphan girl take over and ruin his plans.

That night he went to the cottage. Josh and Joelle had left, due to the shift change, and he let himself into the house. He was proud of himself for thinking, and planning, ahead when he first dated Ruth. He had made a copy of the key and didn't have to break in.

The guardian angels that were watching Hannah during the night, tried to stop him from coming in, but four evil angels appeared. They attacked the guardian angels and locked them into Hannah's bedroom.

Hannah was still up watching the New Year's Eve celebration on TV, when a noise made her turn around. She got up and tip-toed towards the front door.

When Hannah noticed who it was, she turned around to get to her phone, but he grabbed her. She kicked and screamed and tried to get away from him, but he put his hand over her mouth and pushed her forward towards the living room door. When she continued to fight him he hit her across the face to silence her.

The young girl fell backwards, hit her head on the door frame and passed out.

When Joseph saw that Hannah was unconscious, he relaxed. Since Hannah's forehead was bleeding badly, he went into the bathroom to get a bandage. He attended her gash and carried her outside to his car.

Jade and Crystal saw him leave. Their human lived close to Hannah's cottage, and they were about to return to the Guardian Angel Agency when they saw what was going on. They tried to stop him by calming him down, but had no influence on him. Two evil angels appeared, attacked the two female angels and pushed them towards the park. Joseph disappeared without them seeing where he went.

Joseph put Hannah, who was still unconscious, in his car. He gagged her and tied her up, so she couldn't attack him when she woke up. He stepped back and closed the door. When he turned around, he just about had a heart attack when he looked into the dark, angry eyes of Henry Martin.

***

Henry always walked passed Hannah's cottage every night to make sure she was safe and everything locked and closed. Ever since she told him she lived there by herself, he couldn't rest until he had checked on her at night.

He had been on his way back to the homeless shelter when he heard Hannah screaming. He didn't know how many intruders there were, so he kept listening.

When Joseph came outside carrying Hannah, Henry followed and was right behind him when he turned around.

***

"I knew you were scum. I knew the moment we ran into each other in Mrs. Smith's office." Henry's deep voice sounded intimidating but Joseph didn't feel threatened.

"GO home beggar! Oh wait, you don't have a home." He laughed, but before he could do anything Henry's fist hit his face. He tumbled backwards, but caught himself and slammed his own fist into Henry's stomach knocking the air out of him. As Henry doubled over, Joseph punched him again with so much force, that Henry fell to the ground and hit his head on the pavement losing consciousness.

Henry's guardian angels tried to take action, but more evil angels appeared and pushed the guardian angels back, away from the crime scene and behind Hannah's cottage.

Joseph glanced around to make sure nobody had seen the incident, but the neighbours celebrated the holiday in their homes and nobody had witnessed the encounter.

He grabbed Henry by the arms, pulled him away from the curb and into the few bushes behind Hannah's cottage. There he dropped Henry, went back to his car and drove away.

Right after Josh and Joelle had returned to the agency, and once Jade and Crystal had gotten rid of the evil angels, Jade sent a message to Josh to let him know what happened. They returned to the cottage and met with the other angels.

***

"Did you see where he went?" Jo asked as soon as she appeared.

Both shook their head. "No we didn't. The moment we tried to get involved two evil angels appeared and attacked us so we couldn't focus on Hannah." Jade was furious. She hated nothing more than not being able to do her job. It made her feel like a failure.

"Did you contact any other angels?" Josh asked looking at Jade.

"I tried contacting the orphanage here in Edinburgh, but no response so far. The evil angels are blocking our attempts to communicate with other guardian angels."

Jade clenched her fist, ready to explode.

Joelle was shocked that this was even possible. They couldn't even get the police involved since they didn't want to accuse Joseph of something when Ruth still considered him innocent.

Plus they couldn't report him without the truth about Hannah coming out and her losing her place.

"We have to find her." Josh tried sending messages to other angels, but no response.

Suddenly Henry's guardian angels appeared. They got rid of the evil angels and now looked for their human.

"Have you seen Henry? Do you know where he is?" They looked worried.

Just then they heard someone moaning. They turned around to check the bushes behind them and saw it was Henry.

Jade, Crystal, Joelle and Josh made themselves visible with the other two angels staying the way they were.

Joelle knelt next to Henry. "What happened to you, Henry?"

"Jo? What are you doing out here in the middle of the night?"

He sat up and held the back of his head. A big gash was bleeding severely and so the four angels helped him up, and led him into Hannah's cottage and sat him down on the couch.

Jade, who used to be a nurse during her human life, went into the bathroom and found bandages, needles, thread, alcohol and everything else she needed to treat the injury.

"We have to go find Hannah." Henry tried to get up, but Joelle and Josh gently pushed him back onto the couch.

"We will find her, don't worry. First, we need to make sure you're okay."

Jade returned and when Henry saw the things in her hands, he nearly collapsed again.

"You are not going to stitch that up yourself, right?"

Jade grinned. She loved the expression on humans' faces when she did something so unexpected.

"That gash needs stitches right away. I happen to be a nurse so don't worry. We can take you to the hospital though if you'd rather go there."

He shook his head. "We don't have time for that. Hannah is in danger and you blokes need to find her. We can't call the police or else they'll know Hannah is an orphan living here by herself. You're agents aren't you?"

He looked at them and they nodded.

"Do what you have to do."

Jade smiled again and asked Joelle and Josh to hold Henry while she took care of his injury.

Jade worked fast. She cut away the hair around the gash, and cleaned the area with alcohol. Henry breathed through his teeth. It burned liked fire. He didn't move an inch though, and so she stitched it up quickly. She was done in minutes. Once she finished, she gave Henry pain reliever, and he leaned back feeling exhausted.

He looked at Jade.

"Thank you."

"Any time." She smiled.

"So what will happen now?" Henry asked closing his eyes, but he couldn't rest knowing Hannah was still in danger.

"Josh and I will try to find Hannah, and Jade and Crystal will stay with you. We'll let you know once we've found her so you three can go to the police to report this."

"What about Hannah's cottage?"

"Leave that information out for now. We can't let Joseph get away with this. He needs to be punished."

Henry nodded and Josh and Joelle left the room and made themselves invisible.

***

"Josh we need to let Ruth know."

"Yes, but we can't accuse Joseph of it. She has to figure that out herself."

Joelle nodded, but she was angry. She hoped he wouldn't hurt Hannah more than he already had.

***

While Joseph drove through Dunfermline, one guardian angel recognised him. The angel received Josh's earlier message for a split-second and erased the memory in Joseph's head where he had found Hannah.

As soon as he was done, four evil angels came out of nowhere and attacked him and his partner so he couldn't do anything else.

Hannah was awake now, trying to loosen the ropes, but couldn't move. Her head throbbed, and she most likely had a small concussion.

Every so often Joseph smiled at her and it made her angry. It took an hour to drive all the way to Perth.

He drove through the city and stopped right in front of a hospital. He shut off the car, got out, untied her hands and legs, ungagged her, grabbed her by the arms and dragged her with him. She screamed, kicked and tried to get away from him.

When Hannah noticed that he had taken her to a children's psychiatric hospital she threw a huge temper tantrum. She became so wild, he had trouble holding her.

Joseph wanted to beat her for behaving this way, but he had to keep his cool if he wanted the hospital staff to believe him.

He reached the doors and two nurses approached them.

"LET ME GO. LET ME GO!" Hannah screamed, still trying to get away from him. He let go, and she dropped to the floor. She stopped throwing her fit, got up and stepped away from him.

"He kidnapped me and brought me here. You need to call the police."

The nurses looked from one to the other, trading confused looks.

Joseph shook his head.

"She has no idea what she's talking about. I found her…" he couldn't remember. *What happened? Why can't I remember where I found her?* Anyway, I found her on the street. She looked homeless, so I told her I could take her to the nearest police station for help, but she didn't respond and instead fought me, screamed and threw a tantrum. During her fit she stumbled and hit her head on a lamppost next to my car. I decided it was best to bring her here first to make sure she's okay."

Joseph looked at Hannah with so much superficial sadness and pity, it made Hannah sick to her stomach.

"He's lying. He attacked me and forced me to come with him. He hit me and I hit my head on a door. He's dating the woman that takes care of me and he doesn't want her to spend time with me." Hannah gave him a furious look.

Joseph smiled a fake sad smile and looked at the nurses.

"See, she's beside herself."

Hannah couldn't believe that someone could be so superficial and dishonest.

Are the nurses going to believe him?

The older nurse gave the younger one a quick look, and the young nurse nodded and took Hannah by the hand.

"Come with me," the young nurse said and pulled Hannah along with her.

"NO! He's a liar! Why won't you believe me?"

Hannah was shocked that this was happening to her. She tried to get away from the nurse, but the young woman was strong. She noticed how other nurses in the reception desk area glanced at her as if she had gone mad and needed help.

She gave up her resistance and followed the nurse. There was no use. She was stuck and nobody would ever let her out of here again, let alone believe her.

***

The older nurse looked back at Joseph.

"It was a good decision to bring her here. We'll take care of her now. Thank you for looking out for her. Before you leave though, I need your full name and contact number?"

"I'm just the one that found her. Why do you need my information?" Joseph asked the older nurse as he looked down at her, confused.

"We have to check things," she responded "it's the child's word against yours."

He didn't like her response, she could tell. When he turned around to leave, she stepped in his way.

"Not so hasty, Sir! If you're trying to leave now, I must assume that the child is telling the truth and we must call in security." Her look was firm, and she meant business.

He lowered his head, pretending to be sad, but inside he was ready to explode. Knowing anger and aggression wouldn't get him anywhere, he tried to shake it off.

"I'm sorry. I panicked because I've been accused of dishonesty before and it hurts me that anyone would think of me that way. I wanted to help the child. I can't bear the thought of seeing her alone out there. It is winter and freezing."

The nurse nodded and smiled at him.

"I understand. We need more people like you, but running off will not solve problems. I need your name and phone number in case there are further questions."

"Okay, that's understandable. My name is Martin McCormick." He gave her a wrong name and an old phone number.

The nurse thanked him and he left right away. She watched as he drove away.

***

"I'm not lying. Please believe me."

Hannah's whole life fell apart when the young nurse pulled her through the corridor and into a small room.

The nurse put her finger to her lips.

"Shh, I believe you. Can you tell me which car is his?"

Hannah was confused. *Why did the nurse care about his car?*

"Quick, tell me which car is his."

Hannah looked out of the window and pointed it out, and the nurse repeated it into a walkie-talkie.

The young nurse sat down and smiled at her.

"I'm Miranda. What's your name?"

Hannah didn't know what to think, and she didn't trust her.

"What's going on?"

"I said I believe you, sweetie."

"But why?"

Miranda sighed. Before she could respond, the older nurse walked in.

"Did Steven get it?"

Miranda nodded. "I think so."

The older nurse turned around to look at Hannah.

"We believe you because we work for an agency like the one Joelle and Josh work for."

Hannah let out a sigh of relief.

"Did you tell them I'm here? Will they come and get me?"

The older nurse smiled. "We haven't told them yet. We wanted to make sure Joseph was gone first."

She turned to Miranda. *That man is the most horrible actor. I don't think he could even fool humans with his poor performance skills,* the older nurse thought as she shook her head in disbelief and disgust.

Miranda smiled. *I agree, Olga! As soon as he walked in he seemed dodgy.*

Hannah looked from one to the other.

"Can we prove that Joseph kidnapped me?"

Olga smiled again. "If Steven, one of our male security agents, took a picture of the inside of Joseph's car, we can."

A young tall dark haired man entered the room.

"I managed. That git had her tied up in the car," he said clenching his fist.

Miranda and Olga nodded and turned once again to Hannah.

"Let's attend your gash and make sure it heals, then we'll contact Josh and Joelle."

It was past 11:30 pm when Joelle and Josh entered Ruth's block of flats. They went to the third floor and knocked on her door.

It took a while for Ruth to open. She was dressed in her dressing gown and looked like she had been asleep.

"Jo, Josh? Has something happened?" She looked worried.

"Yes," Jo answered. "Someone kidnapped Hannah tonight."

"NO!" Ruth turned pale. Her thoughts went to Joseph, but she didn't want to say it out loud. "Did anyone see it happen?"

"Two of our friends and Henry Martin did, but they didn't see where he went."

"Henry Martin saw the kidnapping? Why didn't he do anything?"

The accusing tone in Ruth's voice made Joelle's blood boil, but before she could snap, Josh answered.

"He tried, but was knocked unconscious."

"That's terrible. Is he okay?" Ruth's eyes were wide with shock, but she blushed ashamed because she was still judging him.

"He's fine. Our two agent friends are with him right now and one of them is a nurse. She stitched up his gash."

"Thank goodness. But what about Hannah, will we be able to find her?"

"Yes we will." Joelle looked into Ruth's eyes, calming her down.

"Should I call the police?"

"Wait until we've found her and have more evidence as in who did it." Josh chose his words carefully.

Ruth looked at them sternly, but felt sick to her stomach.

"We know who did it. I should have never trusted Joseph."

***

It wasn't until around 2:00 am when Josh got word that Hannah was at the psychiatric hospital in Perth.

Steven, and a few other security angels, forced the evil angels away from the hospital so Olga and Miranda could send out a message to Josh and Joelle.

Ruth had fallen asleep on the couch and the two angels didn't want to wake her.

Josh responded straight away asking the three angels at the hospital if they could continue to look after Hannah.

They responded that it was fine since Hannah was asleep too.

When Ruth woke up, Josh and Joelle were still there.

"Did you two sleep? I am sorry I didn't even think about offering you a bed or mattress."

"We're fine, Ruth. We rested too. We know where Hannah is."

Ruth was wide awake. "You do? Where is she? Is she okay?"

"She's just fine," Josh responded with a smile. "She's at the children's psychiatric hospital in Perth."

"WHAT? He took her there?" She got up furious and dialled Joseph's phone number, but only got his answering machine.

"You are the biggest scum on earth, Joseph Walker. How dare you kidnap Hannah and take her to a mental institution? Consider our engagement over. I don't want to have anything to do with you anymore, but you'll regret this, I promise." She hung up, got dressed and the three of them went to Perth to pick up Hannah.

**

Joelle and Ruth sat in the front seats of Ruth's car, and Josh in the back pretending to be asleep, so the two women could talk. Ruth was very quiet.

"Are you okay, Ruth?"

"I feel awful. I let Joseph enter my life and he almost destroyed everything. I didn't realise how much that sweet child meant to me until last night. I hope she'll trust me again at some point. I know she's hurt that I took his word over hers, and she won't trust me for a while. But when we get back to Edinburgh, I'll take her to the orphanage and have them put me down as her foster mum."

Joelle smiled. "Really?"

"Yes. I should have never gotten engaged to that horrible, selfish git and should have listened to Hannah instead and what she tried to tell me. I hope that Hannah can forgive me at one point."

"I am sure she will, but yes you might have to regain her trust. She is hurt."

"I heard your conversation yesterday and called Joseph and cancelled our plans for tonight. I never would have guessed he was as bad as this. I mean it is shocking that he would kidnap Hannah to get her out of my life. I will report him to the police and that's it. I don't want to have anything to do with him ever again."

Joelle swallowed hard, wondering if this was a good time to bring up what he had done to her. But if he did this to other women, Ruth needed to know. He needed to be charged for sexual harassment as well.

"Kidnapping isn't the only thing he did," Jo mumbled.

"What else did he do?" Ruth looked at Joelle terrified, feeling embarrassed that she had seen none of the warning signs.

Joelle told her about the night at the cottage and what happened at the park. Ruth couldn't believe her ears. It made her feel awful that she had put Hannah and Joelle in so much danger.

"Why didn't you tell me?"

"I didn't want to make matters worse. You got so defensive with anything we brought up against Joseph, I didn't think it to be wise to add fuel to the fire."

"I am so sorry, Jo. I am sorry you had to go through that. I hope he didn't traumatise you?"

"I am fine, but figured you should know in case other women got attacked and harassed by him."

Ruth looked at Joelle.

"I don't think I can ever trust a man after this." She tried to sound calm and casual while saying it, but Joelle noticed the disappointment and pain in Ruth's voice. Ruth wasn't an emotional person, but Joelle could tell that she was close to tears.

"We have to be careful, but not everyone is like Joseph," Joelle whispered thinking of Henry.

"I don't know, Jo. I took a long time to open up after my husband passed away, and look how I got burned. Joseph abused my trust, went behind my back, and tried to get rid of a child that meant so much to me."

"Give it time, Ruth. Joseph was not the right one."

***

The psychiatric hospital was packed with talented angels that had special powers. Not only could they read human minds, but they could make them tell the truth if needed.

Miranda and Olga knew from the beginning that something was wrong with Joseph. When they read his mind, it confirmed their assumptions. As an angel in such a special hospital they had the ability to read anyone's mind, even those with the typical evil angel fog or clouds in their head.

***

At the hospital, Hannah slept well. Steven, Miranda and the older nurse Olga, watched over her and made sure that nobody found her. It was hard for evil angels to get into the hospital, so she was safe.

***

Later that morning Hannah was overwhelmed with joy when Josh and Joelle entered the hospital, but as Ruth walked in, her expression changed to resentment and anger.

"Hannah, I am so sorry that I didn't believe you. I should have known better. Joseph tricked me and I know it probably hurt your feelings. I've reported him to the police and broke off our engagement."

"You hurt me, Ruth. I can't believe you took his word over mine."

"I know Hannah, it was a mistake, and I'm sorry. Please forgive me. I promise I will never do something like that again. To show you how serious I am, I've decided to be your new foster mum and move into the cottage with you. Only, if you're okay with it."

"Really?"

Ruth nodded.

Hannah hesitated for a moment not knowing whether to be angry and hurt, or believe and trust Ruth again to give her another chance. As Ruth opened her arms, Hannah swallowed her bad feelings, stepped forward and hugged her motherly friend. Both had tears in their eyes.

Jo smiled, tearing up, and Josh put his arm around her to show how proud he was of her.

They drove to the orphanage and spoke with Mrs. Carter. Ruth filled out a lot of paperwork and told Mrs. Carter everything. She told her she had known Hannah was at the cottage, but hadn't reported her to gain her trust and to make her feel safe.

Since Ruth was a lawyer and well-known in Edinburgh, Katherine Carter accepted everything without making a fuss. She knew Ruth cared about the safety of children, and trusted her in whatever decision she made.

Hannah left with Ruth right away and they would finish the formalities as soon as the information from Hannah's lawyer arrived.

Ruth contacted the lawyer in London, and he promised to get everything ready.

***

Together with Josh and Joelle, they moved a few of Ruth's belongings into the cottage. They didn't need to add much since the cottage was fully furnished and Ruth wanted to either sell her place or rent it out.

Both Ruth and Hannah were excited to start their new life together.

Joseph Walker was furious when he listened to his voicemail and heard the message Ruth left for him. But it got even worse when two police officers showed up on his doorstep, and arrested him. He tried to assure them he had done nothing wrong, but the charges against him said differently.

***

Ruth knew she had to enrol Hannah in school again, so she took Hannah to the secondary school closest to their new home. When they approached Bortonmuir High School, it looked intimidating to Hannah. The building seemed unfriendly on the outside, old and dark, but the inside of the school was the opposite, and Hannah relaxed as they entered.

The headmaster was kind and inviting. He assured her that even though she had not been in school for so long, he knew she would catch up. He tested her in various subjects and confirmed his earlier assumptions. Ruth and Hannah both liked him.

Since the winter holidays were almost over, they decided it would be best if Hannah started school right away.

Headmaster McCormick introduced Hannah to her future teacher, and she too was kind. Hannah liked her from the start.

Mrs. Susan Montgomery was a young lady, in her early twenties, and had the right touch for children starting their teenage years.

Hannah was excited to start school, and Ruth was pleased that things worked out so well.

Joelle and Josh followed them everywhere, even though they were invisible. Joelle was happy that Ruth and Hannah had each other.

They both felt joy again and things were looking better.

Hannah and Ruth got along great and loved each other's company. The orphanage checked in on them, but they had no reason to be concerned.

12. Illegal Activity Behind Closed Doors?

Joseph Walker bailed himself out of prison, which made Josh and Joelle suspicious. Where did he get the money from?

One night, after they left the cottage, they saw him walking through the park. Joseph hurried along the pathway and disappeared into the shadows of a few big trees.

Since both angels were invisible, they followed him. As they got closer, they noticed he was surrounded by evil angels, but those evil angels hadn't seen Josh and Joelle yet.

The two guardian angels had to communicate with their thoughts.

How can we get closer? Is there any way we can be around them without getting attacked? Joelle looked at her trainer.

Not if they want to keep us from finding out the truth. Joseph is up to something and so they want him to succeed, especially with his trial coming up soon.

Josh's facial expression was concerned.

What if I make myself visible and get caught by Joseph? They won't attack me as long as I am with a human right?

No, they won't, but that is risky, Jo. They will attack me instead and you will be on your own. I won't be able to call for help because once they know of us, they will block the area so I can't send mind messages or receive them.

Hmmm. Joelle thought about that. *What if we called for help already and have the other guardian angels hide somewhere around this park so they can see us, but not be seen? Even if mind messages don't work, two of them could get help physically, right?*

Joelle looked at her trainer wondering what he would say, or think in this case.

That would work, but I don't like the idea of you doing this by yourself. It is dangerous. If the evil angels find out about the other guardian angels, they will call for backup and attack all of us.

But they can't hurt me, so even if that happened, what's the big deal? They can only hold you for so long, right? Joelle didn't understand why he was so worried about her. Wasn't she safe from harm as an angel?

They can't hurt you physically, but they can torture you mentally. Josh looked at her concerned when he observed how puzzled she was.

How can they torture me mentally?

They can capture you, take you to someone you care about, and use a human to torture and abuse that person. It is the worst thing evil angels can do to us guardian angels.

Joelle's reaction depicted plain shock. She had never thought of herself still being vulnerable. That would break her apart. She turned to Josh to tell him that Joseph's doing wasn't worth the risk, when she remembered the power she had used when those evil men tortured that little girl. The evil angels were scared of her because of that power, and so perhaps that was her advantage. With that in mind, she knew it could work out.

Let's try it. Joseph is up to something illegal, and we need to find out what. We need to stop him so he can't hurt anyone else.

Jo, are you sure you want to do this? I can't come to your rescue once the evil angels attack, and they make humans do horrible things to get to you mentally.

He looked deep into her eyes and she swallowed hard. She had to admit the thought of seeing someone tortured scared her, but she had a very strong feeling that this was something she needed to do. Knowing she had a special power gave her the courage to see this through. She wanted to know what Joseph was doing.

I am sure. I will be okay. Call the other guardian angels, tell them what we are planning and how we need their help, and then we can only do our best.

Josh wasn't so sure, but Jo was extremely determined.

He contacted several guardian angels, and they hid all over the park. Paul and Sydney were assigned to get the cops when things got too dangerous and they knew what Joseph Walker was up to.

Together they watched Joseph, and the evil angels, for a while.

When Joelle was about to make herself visible, Josh grabbed her arm.

Wait! You can't be here without a reason. No woman would walk through the park by herself this late at night. It will make him suspicious, and puts everyone around in danger.

I could go running. It won't take much to change my outfit into workout clothes. Would that work?

Josh thought about that and nodded.

Joelle pictured a running outfit and her clothes changed. She even had an IPod with head phones in her hands and a tiny stun gun in the pocket of her jumper.

A Taser? Really? She looked at her trainer and shook her head.

He grinned.

Well, you are going running alone. Preparedness is everything!

***

Joseph Walker stood in the shadows of the trees when he noticed Joelle.

She ran along the path, slowed down, then stopped. She played with her IPod and tried to make it work again when he sneaked up to her.

Joseph looked around, making sure nobody followed her or him, and grabbed her from behind. He covered Joelle's mouth and pulled her with him to the spot he had been standing on.

Jo tried to get out of his embrace, but he had her and wasn't letting go this time. She had to admit; it was creepy to be in such an awful situation, in the middle of a dark park, but it had to be done. Women had to be protected from that man.

When the evil angels recognised Joelle, they turned around to find Josh. A moment later they had him too.

***

"Did you really think it to be a smart idea to run through the park alone at night?"

Joseph had a superior smile on his face. He held her tight to his body, but had let go of her mouth.

"Who said I am by myself?" She shot back.

He looked around feeling unsure, but regained confidence right away.

215

"You will regret that you refused my flirting and affections."

"Refused your flirting and affections? You sexually harassed me. You forced your 'affections' on me. There was nothing to refuse. You treated me with disrespect and contempt. The nerve you have to twist everything. You were unfaithful to Ruth you freaking git!" She snapped.

He aggressively pulled one of her arms behind her back and put his hand over her throat.

"Be quiet, Joelle! Tonight you will learn that men are superior to women, and that you can't go against us without suffering serious consequences. I have a good business deal lined up and you are now an added bonus."

Joelle glanced over to Josh. Joseph's last comment got her worried. *Did that mean he was part of a human trafficking group?*

She tried to get out of his embrace, but he didn't let go. When he kissed her neck, and moved his finger up and down her throat, she had enough. She bumped her head back with all the strength she had.

Cursing, he stumbled backwards holding his nose.

Joelle freed herself, pulled the Taser out of her pocket, held it against his neck and stunned him the very next moment. He fell to the ground, moaning and yelling in pain.

Joelle walked over to the bag Joseph had left on the ground. She crouched down, zipped it open and found twenty fake passports in there. That meant he was associated with forgery, but she still believed he had something to do with human trafficking.

She stood back up and turned around to face Joseph again. He was still on the ground, wailing in agony.

"You will be locked up for a long time, Joseph Walker. I'll make sure of it." She glanced at him furious.

"Don't be so certain, young lady!"

Joelle turned around alarmed. Two tall muscular-looking men stood behind her. One grabbed her stun gun and threw it into the loch as far as possible. The other one grabbed her wrists.

"My, my, my what for a beauty do we have here?"

The guy holding her looked her up and down and his facial expression changed from serious to a sickening smile. He had dark hair and a manly scruffy-looking beard, which made him look intimidating.

The other one looked just as scary with his buzzed head and grim-looking eyes. He turned to Joseph, who stood up.

Joseph's nose was bleeding, and swollen, and the shock waves still hurt.

"Joseph Walker?"

"Yes, that's me."

"Frank Harrison send us to meet with you. I am Donovan Copper and that over there is Connor Matthews. Do you have everything Frank asked for?"

Joseph nodded.

Donovan threw a rope at Connor so he could tie Joelle's hands together.

"I guess you didn't just bring what Frank asked, but a gift as well. He will be pleased when he sees her," Connor said as he tied her wrists together and grinned at her.

"Let me go and get lost!" Joelle tried to appear confident because with three men around it was getting dangerous.

"We can't let you go, Love, you know too much. Besides, Frank has been asking for someone new and fresh, and so you came along at the perfect moment."

Joelle breathed through her teeth. He tried to stroke her face, but she moved her head back.

"Are the passports in here?" Donovan asked as he picked up the bag in front of Joelle's feet.

"Yes, twenty as promised," Joseph replied. He seemed nervous now because these illegal exchanges always made him uneasy. The last thing he wanted to happen was getting caught.

Donovan opened the bag and nodded to Connor who still stared at Joelle.

"Thanks Joseph, you did a wonderful job, as usual. Frank will be happy. Here is the agreed sum for the passports." Donovan handed an envelope to the other man.

Joseph checked it and stuffed it in the pocket of his jacket. He turned back and looked at Connor.

"I got you the girl too. Shouldn't I get compensated for her as well?"

"You will get paid as you always have. That's something you have to discuss with Frank though. Our instructions only included the delivery of the money and bringing back the passports in return," Connor replied before he turned his attention to Joelle.

"And now to you, little lady!" He lifted her chin with his hand so she had to look into his eyes.

She used her arms, despite them being tied together, to push his hand out of the way.

"Don't touch me!" she snapped as she stepped backwards. She didn't get far because she bumped right into Donovan who had stepped behind her.

He embraced her with both of his arms and held her as Connor came closer again. Connor grabbed her face, gentle but firm.

"We will have a lot of fun with you before handing you over to Frank," he said smiling.

Josh tried his best to get away from the evil angels, but they didn't let go.

Joelle squirmed around as much as possible, but that Donovan guy was strong. In fact he held her so firm that she thought he wasn't human anymore. That made her panic. She didn't know if evil angels could make themselves look human, and if they had the same strength guardian angels had. How would she be able to use her power in this position?

Joseph watched her with an evil smirk on his face and stepped closer. He looked forward to seeing Joelle tortured and abused.

Joelle had plain terror written over her face. She looked Connor into his eyes as if she was trying to screen his soul.

Suddenly, and without warning, she collapsed sobbing. Donovan had to support her body now because her legs had given in, but she felt how his arms shifted.

The way he held her now appeared more supportive, and like a hug, rather than someone holding a hostage. His body language signalled comfort and encouragement to her.

Was she imagining things?

Josh, and the other guardian angels around, watched her concerned. They couldn't tell whether this was part of an act or the situation got to her? If that was an act, she was an incredible actress because her emotional outburst came across as real.

Sydney and Paul wanted nothing more than to jump in and get her out of there. They knew they couldn't though. With the evil angels around it was too dangerous for everyone involved.

Joelle kicked herself free, but only for a moment.

Connor grabbed her wrists again.

"Please let me go. I promise I won't tell anyone about this. Please don't do this," she begged as tears ran down her cheeks and she sought eye contact with Connor again.

He didn't appear affected by her emotional outburst.

He looked at her with contempt, arrogance, yet longing desire. The smug grin on his face was sickening. When their eyes met, however, she saw compassion, understanding, and empathy in his eyes. It was only for a second, but it gave her hope.

"How stupid do you think we are? Do you believe we fall for a pathetic performance like that? Tears won't help you now. Give it up Joelle! You are under our control and we will enjoy every minute of it."

He smiled wide when he saw how she continued to fight them. Her panic seemed to grow from minute to minute and so Donovan grabbed her again and held her with both of his arms.

"NO, let me go! I don't want you to do this, please…," she said trying to hold back her tears as she did everything in her power to squirm herself free.

"Not so confident and brave anymore, eh Joelle?"

Joseph had stepped in front of her and brutally grabbed her face so she had to look at him.

"Now you will experience firsthand what men can do to women to get respect and submission!"

His smirk was so disgustingly sickening, it made Joelle furious. She pulled her face away from his hand. Her eyes were as cold as ice when she responded.

"You will never get respect or submission from me, Joseph Walker. You are going to pay for everything you have done, and will rot in jail for a very long time. You are one evil creature and the biggest git I have ever met!"

"I will get respect from you, you arrogant beast," he snapped and raised his hand to hit her across her face.

Before he could do anything to her though, something weird happened.

Donovan pulled her away from Joseph, and Connor grabbed Joseph by his jacket and shoved him backwards.

Joelle was stunned. She could have sworn, she had seen held-back anger in Connor's eyes.

Was there still hope for them? Maybe they weren't evil angels after all?

"What was that for?"

Joseph's anger grew from minute to minute and he wanted nothing more than getting back at Connor. He was intimidated enough not to mess with him though.

"Are you completely mad? Do you know what Frank Harrison will do to us if we bring her to him and she is hurt? He will kill us! Don't tell me you have no idea what Frank's biggest rule is?"

Connor looked at the other man furious, and Joseph was speechless for a moment.

"Frank allows no one to hurt a captured woman before she has been sold. She needs to be unharmed, at least unharmed for everyone to see." Connor breathed through his teeth and Joseph looked embarrassed. "You can't lose control like that, man!"

Joelle wondered what would happen next. Would Connor and Donovan possibly let her go?

She had her answer a moment later.

When Connor turned around, he stared at her with so much aversion, yet clear lust, she felt panicky.

Why am I getting so many mixed messages from Connor and Donovan?

Connor's disdain turned into superiority when he saw Joelle's alarmed expression.

"Unharmed for everyone to see doesn't mean we can't do bad things to you." He pulled her face closer, but before he could kiss her, they heard several clicking noises around them.

Joseph and Connor shot around and Donovan let go of Joelle before he also turned around.

Police officers stepped out of hidden positions, guns ready to shoot.

Connor and Donovan raised their arms in defeat, but Joseph was not willing to let them arrest him. Before anyone knew what was going on, he had a gun in his hand and shot at the cops.

Connor grabbed Joelle by her arms.

"Come, let's go!" He pulled her with him.

Joelle, didn't know what was happening. Why was he pulling her away from the group? Then, horror struck her. He wanted to take her to Hannah so he could torture her.

Until that point she had mostly played along, unsure how bad and evil Connor and Donovan were, or if they were human or evil angels. Their changing behaviour confused her. This new realisation changed everything for her though.

He had just played her to make her feel less worried and hopeful. He was an evil angel!

She stopped and refused to go any further. Connor hadn't expected her to stop and so he let go of her arms.

Joelle ripped the ropes off her arms and was about to turn around when Connor grabbed her wrists again and pulled her towards him.

"NO! I won't let you take me with you. Leave me alone!" She tried to break free, but he held her tight.

He looked over her head and saw that Joseph pointed his gun at Joelle now. Connor pushed her to the ground, and threw himself on her to shield her body with his body.

***

While Joseph pointed his gun at Joelle, two officers sneaked up to him and tasered him with their stun guns. He yelled in pain and was handcuffed a moment later.

***

Joelle had not seen Joseph, and how he wanted to shoot her. When she noticed that Connor's body held her down, she interpreted that as another attack. She pushed him away from her with all the strength she had and jumped up.

Connor, who realised how hysterical she was getting, also jumped up. He grabbed her again and pulled her into his arms.

"Joelle, stop fighting me and hear me out!"

"NO! I don't care if you think you are so strong and powerful, but I will never stop fighting you. I don't care what you do to me, but I will not let you hurt my human!"

She tried to get out of his embrace, but he held her firm. He grabbed her upper arms and tried to make her look at him, but she was so much in panic now that she didn't notice how hard he tried to calm her down.

***

Even though she had put on an act before, this was real and not pretend. The guardian angels around watched her in shock. They had never seen a guardian angel so hysterical before.

Paul wanted to jump in and get Joelle away from Connor, but Sydney grabbed his arm. She said something to him and when he looked at her, shook her head.

Josh too wanted to jump in, but he couldn't as long as the officers were around.

Suddenly it struck everyone why Joelle was so hysterical. She always seemed so tough and confident they had forgotten she was still in her training year. It wasn't easy for her to read certain situations. She was also terrified to see Hannah tortured. She didn't care what happened to her, but she was protective of the people she loved and cared about. She couldn't bear the thought of watching them get hurt.

Josh felt bad. He realised that it was his fault she was so freaked out. If he hadn't made such a big deal about being mentally tortured, she would have a different reaction right now.

***

Connor held Joelle firmly by her upper arms, but she kept trying to shove him away from her.

"Joelle, listened to me! Please just calm down!"

"You are not getting Hannah. I won't let you hurt her. I know you evil angels have your free will too, but I won't let you do anything to her."

"I am not trying to hurt her, just hear me out!"

He gently, but firmly, took her head into his hands and tried to force her to look at him, but she refused to look into his eyes.

She tried to loosened his hands, to get out of his hold, but he had her.

"Joelle," he said softly, "I will not hurt you and I won't hurt Hannah. Please look at me."

Connor sighed relieved when she looked up. As soon as their eyes met, she calmed down a little.

"Donovan and I are not evil angels. We are not here to torture your human," he continued saying in a soft tone, "we are…"

"Copper, Matthews, good job as usual, boys!" The police chief said interrupting as he stepped closer. He held the bag with the passports in his hands.

"No problem, Boss, we were eager to finally stop these criminals!" Donovan replied.

Connor loosened his grip so Joelle could turn her head. She looked at Donovan and the police chief in disbelief, and back at Connor. He still held her head with his hands and continued to stare into her eyes.

"So you are undercover cops?" She asked in a trembling voice. He nodded and moved his hands back to her upper arms.

Before he could say anything else, her body released the pressure of panic, fear and worry and she broke down crying. He caught her as she collapsed and pulled her lovingly into his strong arms. Joelle let it happen and silently cried as he held her.

"Hey, it's okay Jo, it's okay!" Connor gently stroke her head as she leaned against his chest sobbing noiselessly.

"Is she okay? Did Joseph Walker harm her in any way?" The police chief looked worried, but Connor shook his head.

"She is fine. It was just too much for her."

Understandingly the police chief nodded, waved at his men, and they cleared the area.

Connor held her tightly, giving her the chance to let it out and calm down again. At the same time he felt terrible because he realised how much this had affected her.

The evil angels had vanished as soon as the police had Joseph, and so Josh was free again.

Sydney, Paul and the other guardian angels waved at them and disappeared to return to the GAA.

Josh made himself visible and walked over to Connor and Joelle.

Connor waited until Joelle's sobbing had stopped. Only then did he lift her chin and looked into her eyes again.

"Are you okay, Jo?" She nodded and wiped the tears out of her eyes.

Josh had reached them now and pulled Joelle in his own arms. He exchanged a quick worried look with Connor and Donovan, but waited patiently until she could speak again.

She swallowed a few times and turned around.

"So if you are undercover cops, and not evil angels, how come you have the strength of a guardian angel?"

Connor stepped in front of her again, grabbed both of her hands and smiled at her.

"We are guardian angels, Joelle. We live at the GAA as well, but since we work as special agents in the Scottish police force, you don't see us much."

She looked relieved and everything began to make sense to her. That's why it calmed her down earlier when Connor looked into her eyes.

"I never meant to make you intimidated or scared. I hate having to do that. I love my job, but scaring women to do a mission is not my favourite thing to do," he said.

Before she could say anything in return, he winked at her and remarked: "Especially when they are as pretty as you!" She blushed and looked over to Josh.

"I am glad you are part of the police force. Your act as criminals was definitely convincing."

"Are you okay, Jo? Was your first breakdown real earlier, or part of an act?" Josh looked at her concerned and worried.

"I am fine, Josh. I was freaked out, but I thought maybe if I showed real emotions I could figure out how atrocious they were. I wanted to get to them, to force a reaction out of them. I never got a complete evil vibe from them and that confused me. In answer to your question: It was mostly an act."

Mostly! Josh, Connor, and Donovan exchanged a quick look.

"Jo, we are so sorry about everything. I rarely mind these special assignments, but tonight I hated every moment of having to scare and intimidate you. When you broke down crying, after we held you the first time, my heart cringed and I wanted you to know I wasn't evil and heartless. It was so hard not to break character, but we couldn't let Joseph get away. I tried to send a message through my eyes, but I am not sure it worked," Connor said looking at her kindly.

"It worked. I saw compassion, understanding, and empathy in your eyes and that helped me calm down at that moment."

He smiled.

"So how come the evil angels didn't recognise that you are guardian angels?"

"Our special power is that we can make evil angels believe we are human, and that's why we get to do such assignments."

"I am so glad to hear that. I was worried because I thought you were evil angels who had the ability to make themselves look human. I thought you were trying to pull me away to take me to Hannah, and I couldn't let that happen. When Donovan held me so firm earlier, I freaked out and panicked because I thought you would take me somewhere and torture me," she said turning to Donovan.

"At the same time it felt as if you were trying to let me know everything would be okay and I didn't need to worry. I noticed how you repositioned your arms and how the way you held me seemed different. It wasn't so intimidating anymore because it felt like it was your way of showing me you weren't as evil as you made it look."

She rubbed her arms, still feeling nervous and uneasy when she thought about the moment when Donovan held her or Connor pulled her away.

The three men noticed that her eyes still had a worried look. Something wasn't right. She wasn't back to her normal self yet.

***

Joelle hadn't been scared of them physically abusing her. When she thought they were human, she knew her power, and her being an angel, was enough protection. But when she expected Connor and Donovan to be evil angels pretending to be human, that's when it got to her.

***

Donovan turned to her now. "Oh I could tell that you were alarmed and even terrified. I felt awful for having to scare you in such a way, but as Connor said earlier, we had to make sure Joseph, and the evil angels, didn't become suspicious. We had to bring this mission to an end. Joseph was the last one to be arrested, and so we had to be careful.

When you broke down crying, I knew I had to let you know I didn't want to hurt you. I realised I had to do something to make you feel comforted and less terrified without letting the evil angels and Joseph know."

He gently squeezed her hand.

"It was an awful feeling holding you as you collapsed, Jo. It was somewhat disturbing. I never wanted to break character more than at that moment," he added.

Joelle silently sighed because her earlier feelings had been right. She tried to look casual and unaffected, but her relief showed on her face.

Josh pulled Joelle into his arms and looked into her blue eyes.

"Jo, what's wrong?" He had a serious expression on his face. She felt Connor and Donovan staring at her and blushed.

Admitting that she wasn't always tough and strong was hard for her, but she couldn't lie. She looked up to him and didn't know how to share her feelings.

She lowered her head and leaned against his chest.

"I shouldn't be a guardian angel. I am not good at it. Maybe I should just get an assignment in heaven," she whispered more to herself than them.

Josh looked down on her, stunned.

"What are you talking about?"

He lifted her chin and made her look at him.

"Don't you see, Josh? I can't stand the pressure! It was my first real challenge, and I failed. I never had a hysterical breakdown as a human. It isn't in my nature to lose it like that. I should have kept myself in check and didn't. What use am I for a human if I break apart like that? When I volunteered to let myself get caught by

Joseph, I thought I could handle it, but clearly that's not the case. I failed miserably. I put on an act, with the crying and breakdown in the beginning, but I wasn't pretending later on. That was real," she mumbled, lowering her eyes again.

Josh and the other two exchanged an understanding glance. Joelle was disappointed with herself because she believed she shouldn't show weakness.

"The GAA needs angels that are tough and strong, like you three. They need angels that can handle anything, and not someone who breaks apart when a situation becomes more challenging."

Josh gently lifted her chin and made her look at him again.

"Now listen to me, Jo! You are a wonderful guardian angel and exactly like you should be. Heavenly Father created you the way you are for a reason. Men and women are different and that's good. That doesn't mean we are tougher than you are, just different. Women are tough in their own way and just because you show more emotions, does not mean you aren't tough," Josh said looking into her eyes.

"You are a very tough chick," he added, and that made her smile.

"Be grateful that Heavenly Father made it so you can let your emotions out when you've reached your limits. It is harder for us men. Just because we don't show our feelings the way women do, does not mean we don't have those emotions too. It just shows differently, like we are more irritable and angry or down."

Connor and Donovan nodded in agreement and smiled at her kindly.

"You did everything right tonight. Every single situation with Joseph Walker, and Connor and Donovan too, was terrifying. Do you know why you were so affected by it?" Joelle shook her head.

"Because you not only feel your own emotions, but you can sense the feelings of women going through those situations in real life. You know what it must be for them. That has to get to you at one point. You never had a hysterical breakdown as a human because nobody has ever threatened your loved ones like that before, right?" Joelle nodded slowly. She understood what he was trying to say.

"Tell me something, Jo! When you thought Connor was an evil angel, and you became so hysterical, why were you fighting him so much?"

"Because I thought he wanted to take me to Hannah and hurt her."

"Exactly! And that's what a wonderful guardian angel does. You only thought about Hannah and how she would suffer. You didn't care about yourself, but you panicked because you were afraid Connor would do something to her." She looked up, and he smiled at her. She felt better because what he said to her was true.

"It is okay to show fear and worry, Jo. Being angels does not mean we will stop feeling human emotions. You are a strong, determined and brave woman, but also sensitive, compassionate and tender-hearted. Everyone reaches their limits. You can't always be strong, Jo. It isn't a weakness to show your true feelings. It shows how caring and brave you really are. That's why men are created differently. Heavenly Father wants us to be protectors and a strong shoulder to lean on. He knew women would need that because He gave you such strong emotions. That's why I am your partner, why we have partners in general. We help each other through the times when we have reached our limits."

Joelle blushed again, but Connor and Donovan nodded in agreement. The three men couldn't help but think how adorable she looked at that moment. Her sweet bashfulness suited her.

"Thank you, Josh." He wiped hair out of her face and hugged her tightly.

"I meant every word, Jo. Never think you are weak because you feel strong emotions. Your caring heart shows how strong you really are!" She smiled and felt so much better.

***

She was grateful that Josh, Connor and Donovan were so sensitive and understanding. It made her thankful that they had helped her through this without judging her. She realised what for wonderful caring men they were. They understood their role in life and helped her see things with different eyes.

They reminded her of her human father. He was one of those men who had always been there for his wife.

He was strong and protective, but also caring and loving. Her parents completed each other because they knew they were equal, yet unique in their own way.

Joelle had learned from them how important it is to love and accept the role given by Heavenly Father.

They taught her that being a woman was a wonderful thing. She didn't need to be a man to love herself and feel the love from her Heavenly Father.

It made her sad that so many women out there, felt the need to compete with men to prove they were equal to or better than men. They clearly didn't understand what equality really meant, and why Heavenly Father created men and women differently.

Joelle was tough on herself, and didn't want to seem weak, but she had never felt unequal to men. There were some men who treated women badly, and thought themselves above women, but the majority wasn't like that.

Joelle admired men who were strong, protective providers, but treated women with love and respect. A real man does not think of himself as superior to women, but as the other half to one of Heavenly Father's creations.

Josh, Donovan, and Connor would make great husbands to anyone who appreciated and respected them. They were keepers for sure.

***

She noticed how the three men watched her as she disappeared into her own thinking world. When she thought about the whole evening again, their confusing behaviour made sense to her.

"So when Joseph was about to hit me, you two actually tried to protect me from him?"

"Yes. We couldn't let him strike you. I made up the story about Frank and his rule, because I knew I had to be convincing so Joseph would believe me," Connor responded.

"You were angry when he wanted to slap me, weren't you? I thought I saw held-back anger in your eyes," Joelle said as she looked up to him.

"I was furious. I almost broke character at that moment, and wanted to rip his head off. It made me so angry that he treated a woman with such arrogance and disrespect. If he would have attempted to hurt you one more time, I would have lost it," Connor said as he clenched his fists.

Joelle gently touched his arm and when he looked at her, calmed him down. She felt touched that these three tough-looking, strong men were so protective of her.

They did what they could to keep her safe, even if they had to freak her out and confuse her repeatedly.

"And why did you pull me away from Joseph and the other cops? Couldn't you have just told me you were a guardian angel?"

Connor shook his head.

"I pulled you away from the police officers and Joseph, because I tried to get you away from the evil angels. I didn't think it would make you freak out more. I couldn't tell you right there and then, because the evil angels didn't know we are guardian angels." That made sense.

"And why did you push me down, Connor, and threw yourself on me?" She looked at him confused and he grinned.

"Joseph was pointing his gun at you, and I tried to protect you in case he would have fired a shot."

"But it wouldn't have made a difference. He can't inflict wounds on us guardian angels."

"I know that, but Joseph didn't know we aren't human and so I needed to make it look like I was trying to cover your body with mine. I am sorry if it seemed like I was attacking you. Right after I threw you to the ground, the cops overpowered him."

"Who was Joseph working for?" Joelle asked.

"He worked for a human trafficking ring. They sold fake passports illegally, and abducted women and children to sell to wealthy men and harlots. The passports were given to sex offenders on probation, so they could leave the country and start a new life as someone else and continue their evil lifestyle. It took the police a few years to sort this out, but tonight they busted everyone."

"So Joseph abducted women and children as well?"

"No, but as we saw tonight, he would do it if he gets the chance."

Joelle shivered as she thought about what women and children had to go through.

Josh pulled her back into his arms and gave her a hug. He kissed her forehead before letting her go again.

"Oh and thanks, Josh, you played your part well and convincing," Donovan said as he patted Josh's shoulder.

"What do you mean by Josh played his part well?" Joelle shot around and gave her trainer a killing stare.

"Well, we contacted him because we knew this mission would go smoother if Joseph had a hostage person around. It made our part much more believable and him less worried."

"So you set me up?" Joelle's facial expression became irritated.

"Yes. I knew if we walked through the park, and you saw Joseph Walker, you would want to take action. I know how determined you are when you have your mind set on something, and so I figured it to be the best solution."

"Oh you figured, eh?" Joelle looked at her trainer, and it was clear that she was not happy with him.

"In Josh's defence, we needed a female angel still in her training year, and who had been harassed by Joseph before," Connor said, trying to calm her down again.

"And why is that?" Jo raised an eyebrow as she turned to Connor now.

"Because in order for us to be believable, and not alarm the evil angels, we needed someone who couldn't tell right away that we are guardian angels. Your confusion confused them. As police mission agents, we have the power to mislead evil angels. We can make them believe we are human, and they still in charge, but only if we can deceive guardian angels. Fully trained angels can't be fooled by us anymore, but those in training can. Your worry and confusion showed on your face, and so the evil angels assumed that we were human. They thought we had received our strength from our guardian angels, who had become evil."

"And why did you use me for that?"

"Because you do what it takes to get justice. You are a firm believer in fairness, and wanted Joseph to get punished for everything he did. You knew him, and we believed you could handle it even if Connor and Donovan freaked you out. I should have never scared you with what the evil angels can do to us guardian angels. If I hadn't said that, you would have reacted differently."

Josh put his arm around her shoulders, but Joelle stepped away from him. She enjoyed her part now in making them think she was mad at them. Guilty suffering was good for them.

"You still should have told me. It was unfair and rude, to use me in such a way. Pretending you cared for my well-being by not wanting me to do this, yet you plotted this mission and were counting on me to do this no matter how dangerous it was. You willingly sacrificed me, and my determination for fairness, to get what you want. Do you even realise what you put me through? Do you have any idea how traumatising this was?" She looked at them hurt and offended and then turned around to walk away.

Josh, Connor and Donovan stepped in her way.

"We didn't mean to hurt or offend you, Jo. We knew if anyone could handle such a difficult situation it would be you. We never meant to frighten, intimidate or make you scared, but we had to be convincing to make sure the evil angels believed us. We never intended to get to you in such a torturing way."

She enjoyed seeing them feel guilty. As freaked out as she had been earlier, she was back to her normal cheeky self and saw nothing wrong with getting them back.

Joelle silently looked at them for a few minutes, just standing there. She tried her hardest to keep a straight face, but suddenly burst out laughing.

"So you were just messing with our poor emotions?" Josh asked in an intimidating tone of voice.

She nodded, stepping away from them slowly.

"Just you wait!" Josh called out and the three of them walked towards her with a mischievous grin.

She turned around to make a run for it, but didn't get far. Connor reached her first, turned her around and threw her over his shoulder.

"Connor, put me down!"

"No, way. You made us feel horrible, and that means punishment," he responded grinning.

"What shall we do with her?" Donovan asked winking at the other two.

"Hmm, let's see. We could stay visible and carry her to the GAA."

Connor got a kick out of this situation. Jo wiggled around to get off his shoulder, but he held her firm.

"Don't you dare! Please, just put me down."

"We could also make her blush. When Jo first met me, she was so taken by my attractive manliness she willingly shared her thoughts with me so I would know she finds me handsome!"

Connor and Donovan laughed.

"You are unbelievable Josh McIntosh!" She kicked Connor's chest to have him let her down, but he continued to laugh.

"Maybe we can get into her thoughts and find out what she thinks about us. She might find us just as handsome and manly," Connor said.

"You better put me down this instant, or…" she replied before she stopped herself

"Or what?" Josh raised an eyebrow.

"… or I will never talk to you again. You are being totally unfair. Three grown men against a girl? Not very handsome or manly."

"The best way to handle this is to make her pay ransom for her freedom. We should demand a kiss from her."

Donovan and Josh laughed out loud. Joelle rolled her eyes but blushed greatly.

Connor took her of his shoulder and stared at her with a straight face.

"So? What do you think, Jo? Is that a fair offer?"

"If you think I will kiss any of you because you play this mean game with me, and use your manly angel strengths against me, you are mistaken." She too kept a straight face, and looked into his eyes without blinking, but blushed.

"That's not the way I see it. I believe I deserve a kiss, considering I never got to kiss you earlier. I feel cheated. If the police chief had only waited a minute longer…" he said looking into her eyes. Joelle blushed again, but before she could respond he continued: "by the way, you look adorable when you are embarrassed."

He winked at her and gave her a winning smile.

"You guys are so mean! Do you do that with every girl you meet, you know putting her on the spot?" She tried to ignore her embarrassment, but her cheeks were still bright red.

"We only do that with the cute ones!" Connor replied.

She rolled her eyes and stepped away from him, but he pulled her back into his arms.

"We are only teasing you because of your charming and enchanting reaction."

"Well, you better stop saying things like that, just to make me blush, or my reaction will not be enchanting and charming for much longer!" She looked up to him and he gave her a brotherly hug.

"You do know hugging can be considered as harassment, right? I mean we just met. What makes you think you can get away with this?" Joelle asked with a raised eyebrow after he let her go.

"I figured since you consider Josh handsome, and he gets to hug you, you see us that way too."

"You are impossible, all three of you!" She elbowed Connor in his stomach, but it only made him laugh more. He pulled her back into his arms.

"Friends?"

"Okay, fine, but you making me blush has to stop!"

"As you wish, my lady!" Connor responded with a grin as he bowed down. Joelle just rolled her eyes and shook her head.

They returned to the GAA, and Josh lovingly pulled her into his arms before they said their goodbyes. When she stepped away from him, Connor and Donovan opened their arms.

"What about us?" Connor grinned, and winked at her. She smiled back.

"Okay fine, you can hug me too," she replied with a dramatic sigh and eye roll. It made them laugh.

Donovan hugged her first, and then it was Connors turn to pull her into his arms. He bear-hugged her and even lifted her off the ground before setting her down with a grin. They said goodnight to each other and separated.

***

Connor and Donovan weren't on their team, but Joelle liked their easy going personality and was hoping to work with them again. It surprised her that they had teased her so quickly, but no matter how much she had blushed, their teasing hadn't felt uncomfortable to her. She had always enjoyed friendships with boys, and Connor and Donovan seemed to be like Josh. She had felt weird and freaked out around them, but only in the beginning. Paul was the only angel, so far, who had made her truly uncomfortable and nervous.

13. A Trial of Justice!

Joseph Walker's trial began a few weeks after Hannah started school. His trial was split into two parts. The first day was about the kidnapping, and sexual harassment. The second day was about his involvement with illegal activity, like forgery and working for the human trafficking ring.

Since Joelle had to testify in both cases, she had to appear at both trials.

Ruth hired her colleague Kate Harris. Kate was a fantastic prosecutor and since Ruth pressed charges, she knew she couldn't be the prosecutor herself. Kate worked hard to put the pieces together.

Joseph himself hired John Hamilton, who was a vicious defence lawyer, and was certain he would get through this trial with no negative consequences.

Ruth knew John Hamilton too, but didn't feel intimidated. During the past few weeks Kate and her, had prepared their case well. They had several witnesses, including Henry Martin, and were determined to show Joseph and John that dishonesty does not pay.

Joelle had brought Jade and Crystal to the trial, and the three special angels from the hospital in Perth.

A few evil angels tried to get into the building, but Josh, who was still invisible, and a few other guardian angels, kicked them out. They made sure there was a special protective shield around the whole building, which made the evil angels furious.

The judge entered the room and everyone stood up. As soon as he took his place, everyone was seated again.

Joseph glanced at Ruth and Hannah, but they ignored him.

Hannah was beckoned to come forward and sit in the witness stand. Kate asked her to tell the court what she remembered about the night of the kidnapping.

Hannah shared her experience, and then John Hamilton approached her.

"Isn't it true you disliked Mr. Walker from the beginning, Hannah?" She gave him a cold glance.

"I was guarded with him. He made it clear that he didn't like me, and didn't want me around, so yes I wasn't too keen on him."

"But weren't you hoping for Mrs. Smith to adopt you?"

"What does that have to do with anything?"

"Well, if you were hoping for adoption, and did not want to share Mrs. Smith with Mr. Walker, you have a good reason to lie."

"Objection your Honour, Mr. Hamilton is putting words into the mouth of this witness and is trying to intimidate her." Kate stood up.

John Hamilton looked at her angrily.

"Sustained! Mr. Hamilton, please abstain from accusations and intimidations when questioning a witness."

The judge gave the defence lawyer a warning look before he turned to Hannah.

"Hannah, you don't have to answer that."

"I would like to though," she replied and looked squarely at John Hamilton.

"You can try to twist it as much as you like, Sir. It will not change that Mr. Walker kidnapped me, beat me and took me to a mental hospital."

Shocked at her sincere and direct response, Mr. Hamilton didn't know what to say. Hannah was released and Sydney and Paul, who took care of Hannah during the trial, took her outside.

Kate addressed the judge and jury once again.

"We have pictures and a written report, showing the conditions in which Hannah Spencer was brought to the hospital in Perth. Not only had Mr. Walker tied her up in his car, the nurses had to attend a bleeding gash on her forehead just as Miss Spencer had mentioned."

Kate looked at Joseph with a grin and handed the information and evidence to the judge. He studied everything and passed it on to the jury.

Joseph jumped up in anger.

"That's a lie! Those reports are falsified."

"Mr. Hamilton please keep your defendant from interrupting." The judge gave John Hamilton an angry look, who turned to Joseph in frustration.

Joseph sat down.

"You will have your chance to defend yourself," John hissed to his client.

Kate Harris stepped forward again and called another witness. "I'd like to call Mrs. Marianne Gilmore to the witness stand."

Joseph's face turned pale. He turned around and saw a middle aged woman coming down the aisle. Her long black hair was in a ponytail, and she avoided looking at Joseph.

"Mrs. Gilmore, is it true you and Mr. Walker have been dating for six months?"

She nodded. "That is correct."

"Did you know he was dating a second woman, and was engaged to her, during the same six months?"

The jury members whispered with each other. Many made notes, and the audience shook their heads.

"No I didn't."

For the first time, Marianne looked at Joseph and her eyes showed disgust. She couldn't believe his lies and the games he had played with her.

"When did you find out?"

"When Mrs. Smith contacted me and told me."

The whispering became louder.

"Did you believe her right away?"

"No I didn't."

"What made you change your mind?"

"I changed my mind when two police officers came by and asked me if Mr. Walker had been with me the night of the kidnapping. He had used me as his alibi."

"What did you tell them?"

Marianne looked at Joseph. "I told them it was true."

Joseph released a silent sigh.

Kate smiled at the other woman.

Marianne kept her eyes on Joseph, enjoying the moment.

"I told them he had indeed been with me, but he didn't get to my place until after midnight. I had not seen him, or heard from him, during the time of the kidnapping."

Everyone whispered now, and it took a few minutes until it was quiet again.

Joseph sank back into his seat turning pale again, and his lawyer shook his head.

Kate walked back to her seat.

"Your witness Mr. Hamilton." She grinned, but he waved his hand. Ruth smiled. Kate called another witness.

"I am now calling Mr. David Camden to the witness stand."

Now even Ruth was surprised and Joseph felt sick to his stomach.

David Camden, a small bald man with thick glasses sat in the chair on the witness stand.

John, who was getting angry now, leaned over his chair.

"Who is that, Mr. Walker?"

Joseph closed his eyes. "My former boss."

"Mr. Camden, Mr. Walker worked for you, is that correct?" Kate asked as she stood in front of the witness.

"Yes."

"How long did he work for you?"

"He worked for me for ten years."

"Why doesn't he work for you anymore?" Kate watched him as he glanced toward Joseph for a split-second.

"Because I caught him stealing money from me."

The jury whispered again, and Ruth and Marianne, had to gasp for air.

"How long did he steal from you?"

"For a few years."

"What happened when you discovered it?"

"I told him I would report him to the police."

"But you didn't?"

"No, he asked me not to. He said he would give the money back."

"Did he?"

"He did."

Ruth looked at Joseph in disbelief. Marianne thought she was in a bad movie or something. Kate called Marianne back to the witness stand.

"Has Mr. Walker ever mentioned to you that he had lost his job?"

"He mentioned it once. He said one of his colleagues had lied to his boss and that he had lost his job, but he shared no detail."

"Has he ever asked you for money?"

Everyone held their breath.

"Yes. He told me he would lose everything, and that the banks wouldn't give him another loan since he had one for his house and one for his car. He said he struggled to find a new job."

"Did you give him money?"

"Yes, I did."

The jury members and audience whispered again, and Marianne sat back down.

Kate interviewed Ruth now.

"Mrs. Smith, has Mr. Walker ever asked you for money?"

"Yes, right before he kidnapped Hannah, but I never gave him anything."

"During your courtship, did he ever pay your way for anything?"

"He paid for everything. He took me out to supper, the theatre, lunch, the pictures, and other things. So it surprised me when he asked me for money."

Marianne jumped up. "You used my money to date another woman?"

Mumbling and muttering went through the courtroom. The judge had to use the gavel a few times before everyone calmed down again.

Joseph felt horrible, not for what he had done, but because he had been caught.

Marianne was outraged.

Kate released Ruth from the witness stand and called David Camden back.

"Mr. Camden, was the fact that Mr. Walker stole from you the only reason you fired him?"

"No. Right after I found out he had been stealing from me, several of my female employees came forward and claimed they had been sexually harassed by Mr. Walker. After looking into the accusations, I knew I had to let him go to protect my female employees. They didn't want to press charges out of fear of retaliation."

"Mrs. Harris, do you have witnesses to confirm Mr. Camden's statement?"

"I do, Mr. Hamilton. I have the report of his former Co-workers here. They didn't feel comfortable appearing in court. They said they would testify in private in your presence, if needs be, Your Honour!"

The judged nodded and took the reports from Kate Harris. He looked at it and handed it as evidence to the jury.

"Is that all?"

"No, Mr. Hamilton. I have one witness who will testify here in court. I am calling Mrs. Joelle Anderson to the witness stand."

As soon as Joelle was seated, Kate Harris asked her about the incidents at Ruth's home and what happened at the park. Then John Hamilton addressed Joelle.

"Mrs. Anderson, my client said you were flirtatious with him and seemed to enjoy the extra attention. If you had a problem with his affectionate behavior, why didn't you put him in his place?"

"It is a lie that I flirted with him. I did not trust him one bit and had no interest in him. When he started his sexual advances, I told him several times to stop. I told him I didn't want to be touched by him, but he ignored those warnings."

"My client also said the only reason he, let's say 'pushed the boundaries a bit', was because he knew you are some sort of agent. He was convinced you would stop it if you thought he was going too far. And clearly, Mrs. Anderson, if you are indeed an agent, shouldn't you be able to defend yourself against unwanted sexual advances? Your inaction is testifying you were okay with it."

Kate Harris jumped up outraged. "Objection, Your Honour!"

"Sustained! Mr. Hamilton that was the second time you questioned a witness out of line. I am not warning you again. Please remember that your defendant is on trial and not the witness."

John Hamilton nodded with gritted teeth. The judge looked at Joelle.

"Mrs. Anderson, you don't have to respond to that."

"I know, Your Honour, but it is important that I do."

She looked at the defence lawyer infuriated.

"Mr. Hamilton, did you just indirectly try to say it is okay to sexually harass me because I am an agent and should be able to defend myself?"

Outraged muttering went through the courtroom. Several jury members looked upset and irritated.

"I never said that!" John Hamilton raised his hands into the air.

"No you didn't, but I can read between the lines. Mr. Walker did not push the boundaries a bit. He forced his sexual advances on me although I repeatedly told him to stop."

The muttering got louder and many looked at John Hamilton and Joseph Walker bothered and annoyed.

"Sexual harassment is wrong, period! It shouldn't matter whether or not a woman can defend herself. If a woman tells you to stop, you stop. No means no and this behaviour, and attitude, is the reason women don't come forward and speak about their experience."

John Hamilton tried to interrupt, but Joelle wasn't done.

"I am the **VICTIM** of sexual harassment and I refuse to be turned into the offender!"

Several people in the audience clapped to support what Joelle had said. The judge used the gavel to get order back into the courtroom, but his facial expression showed that he agreed with everything Joelle had said. He was pleased and proud that she stood her ground so firm and confident.

They had more than enough evidence to show what Joseph Walker was capable of. After the other witnesses had testified, it was Joseph Walker's turn to defend himself.

"Mr. Walker is there anything else that should be shared with this court?" John Hamilton gave Joseph Walker a warning look not to say anything wrong.

"Yes there is." He stared at Ruth with pure disdain, and gave her an evil grin. "That woman over there," he said pointing at Ruth, "is not the honest person she claims to be."

"Mr. Walker, I suggest you speak respectfully of others in the room and refer to them by their name."

The judge rebuked him once again and Joseph Walker had to bite his tongue this time, not to say something rude in return.

"Very well. Mrs. Smith wasn't Hannah's foster mother when she and I dated. She hid the child in the cottage that used to belong to Hannah's parents. She bought the place right before we met, to keep Hannah safe, but she should have handed the girl over to the authorities instead of keeping it a secret."

Some audience members looked surprised, but the judge and the jury members shook their heads.

"Mr. Walker…," the judge began, but was interrupted by Joseph Walker.

"Forgive me, Your Honour, but that is not all. Mrs. Smith left Hannah unsupervised most of the day, and at night, which means she was not concerned about Hannah's safety. If she had been concerned she would have done something about it." He grinned and looked around gloating over his new evidence. He had made an important and trial changing point.

John Hamilton looked pleased. Both Kate and Ruth were outraged, but before they could say anything, the judge addressed the defendant.

"Mr. Walker let me enlighten you at once. I am well aware of the circumstances. Mrs. Smith has informed me of this herself and told me everything before this trial even began. She handled the situation well and did everything she could to help Hannah. It is best to report an orphan, but in this case it was better to leave her where she was instead of having her wander the country." He stopped for a moment before he continued.

"You, however, used the knowledge you had against Hannah's safety. You broke into her home, injured her, and removed her from her safe place. You broke the law and have no right to point your finger at anyone else. Mrs. Smith's intentions were honourable despite what you might say!"

Joseph was shocked and speechless. He had been sure of getting through the trial unpunished, and yet it didn't look good for him. In a last attempt he tried everything to get someone to believe him, but the witnesses, evidence and pictures proved otherwise.

Kate Harris and John Hamilton gave their closing arguments, and the judge closed the trial for the day. He adjourned the trial until the next day and stood up.

Everyone else got up as well, and the jury left the courtroom to start their deliberations.

John Hamilton and Joseph Walker argued while everyone else was leaving the courtroom, and before two officers took Joseph into custody again. Joseph accused John of not being a good lawyer, and John shot back saying Joseph should have been more honest with him from the start.

Henry slipped out of the courtroom as soon as the trial ended. Ruth smiled at Kate and thanked her thoroughly for the great work. Both Kate and Ruth thanked the witnesses for coming, but when Ruth looked around to thank Henry, she couldn't find him.

***

Hannah and Sydney met Joelle and Ruth outside, and Hannah hugged Ruth and Kate. Joelle said her goodbye for the day and they left.

When nobody was around anymore Joelle made herself invisible. Josh gave her a big hug and a high five.

"They did great, Jo. I'm so proud of you too for your part in this whole thing. Things are looking great and I'm certain that Ruth will adopt Hannah before your year of training is over."

"That would be wonderful. Oh Josh, I hope that Joseph gets the punishment he deserves."

"He will. Today's court session did not turn out well for him, and tomorrow will be the same, if not worse. I am proud of you for standing your ground earlier, and I am sure the judge felt the same way even though he won't admit it."

Joelle smiled and Josh put his arm around her again.

"Let's go to the park. I told Steven, Miranda and Olga we would meet them there before they head back to Perth."

***

"Thank you so much for taking such good care of Hannah and looking out for her. How did you know she was kidnapped, and we looked for her? Did Josh's message reach you? I thought the evil angels out there broke off the connections," Jo said looking at the angels.

"We didn't know you were looking for Hannah, but we heard Joseph's thoughts when he walked in and knew something was up. Steven saw the evil angels, and together with a few other angels in the car park, he made sure they were gone."

Olga smiled at Joelle.

"And then we received Josh's message," Miranda told them.

"But can't evil angels get into a psychiatric hospital?" Joelle looked confused.

"Not really, no. A mental institution is a well-protected place. The angels inside and outside, have special powers to protect the humans that are more vulnerable than those who only have physical injuries. The outside angels are in charge of the protective shield, and only on few occasions can an evil angel break through," Steven explained to Joelle.

She understood. "So it's like when an evil angel influences a doctor or nurse outside the hospital and they become evil and bring an angel with them into the hospital?"

"Exactly! It doesn't take long to notice it, but once an evil angel (or even a few) is inside it's hard to kick them out again, and takes a while before we succeed."

Joelle found it fascinating. She felt like asking many more questions, but Olga, Miranda and Steven had to go.

They said their goodbyes, snapped their fingers and poof they were gone.

Joelle and Josh went back to the cottage to keep an eye on Hannah. She was safe since Ruth's guardian angels were around, but they wanted to make sure, and it was still early.

"Could I ever get assigned to a mental hospital or an orphanage?"

Josh smiled. He had read her thoughts earlier and had expected the question.

"We get sent wherever we're needed, Jo. If you're needed in a special place like a hospital, or orphanage, you'll get sent there and you'll receive the powers that come with the job."

"Do they train angels there too?"

"Oh yes they do. Miranda is still in training."

"Do you have to have been a special or perfect human to be sent to the angel agency at a mental hospital?"

Again Josh smiled. He loved that she was so eager to learn, so willing to try new things.

"No you don't have to have been a perfect human, but most of the angels there had mental disabilities as humans. They were sent there since they can relate best to how the humans feel."

When Josh and Joelle arrived at the courthouse the next day, they saw that Connor and Donovan had also arrived.

Connor walked up to Joelle and gave her a big smile.

"It's good to see you again, Jo. I heard you did an amazing job at the hearing yesterday."

"Well, I simply defended myself against that word-twisting defence lawyer."

***

The second trial day went as Josh said it would. There was too much evidence against Joseph Walker.

Joelle was called as a witness again and shared with the court what had happened to her.

The jury left as soon as the trial was over and the judge adjourned the trial to the following day.

***

Josh and Joelle checked on Ruth and Hannah after they said their goodbyes to the two undercover cop guardian angels.

When they arrived at the cottage, they walked right in since they were both invisible. Ruth and Hannah had supper and talked about the day.

The cottage had changed since Ruth moved in, but both loved it. The fireplace was burning, and it was a lovely winter night.

After they finished eating, Ruth made two large cups of hot chocolate. Hannah turned on music, and both snuggled up on the couch enjoying their hot drink.

Joelle and Josh sat down in a corner, enjoying the warmth of the fire when Joelle put her head against the little book case next to her.

"I will miss Hannah, Ruth and all of this."

Josh put his arm around her and pulled her closer.

"You still have a few months ahead of you, don't get sad now."

She rolled her eyes. "I can't help it. Besides, time goes by way too fast."

He couldn't deny that.

"Tell me Josh, will you have to train again?"

"I don't think so. I've trained twice in a row now and have been here in Edinburgh for two years. My guess is that I'll be sent somewhere else this time, with a regular partner and assignment, no trainee."

"I will miss you, Josh." She looked into his brown eyes and he saw a sad smile around her eyes and mouth.

"Jo, believe me, I will miss you too. I've never had such a loving and fun partner before, and it's been a pleasure to tease you, knowing you would never get angry or hurt. But again let's not focus on our farewell, but enjoy the next few months together."

She sighed. "I'll try my best."

***

The next day, all of them met together in court to hear the verdict. Kidnapping a child, forgery, sexual harassment and being involved with human trafficking, weren't crimes they would let Joseph walk away from.

Especially since there were so many witnesses and plenty of evidence.

Everyone stood when the judge entered. The jury handed him an envelope, and he read the verdict. Now it was up to him to decide how to present the punishment Joseph may or may not receive.

"Will the defendant please rise?"

Joseph and his lawyer stood up.

"Mr. Walker," he said. "In the case of Hannah Spencer, the jury has found you guilty of kidnapping, assault and battery. In summary of this court's proceedings: you attacked and kidnapped a child; forced her into a mental institution for your own selfish benefit; lied to and deceived those you associated with; and injured Mr. Martin when he tried to defend the girl. I too declare you guilty and sentence you to two years in prison. I also order you to pay back every single pence you borrowed from Mrs. Gilmore.

Joseph gasped for air.

"Two years?" He shouted, drawing everyone's attention. "She was hardly gone."

"It doesn't matter how long she was gone, you took her, tied her up and took her to a mental institution. You kidnapped a child! Not to mention that you lied, and took advantage of two women. You're lucky that your former boss pressed no charges and let you go." The expression on the judge's face told Joseph he was not willing to discuss the subject any further.

Joseph fell back into his chair. He couldn't believe it.

I got two years because of that stupid orphan? I will not put up with this.

Seeing Joseph's thoughts, made Joelle so angry that she wanted to go over there and slap him across the face.

Connor, who sat next to her, put his arm around her shoulders to hold her back in case she snapped. Josh, who was invisible, calmed her down so she wouldn't do anything stupid.

As she calmed down she heard Jade quietly giggling. Jo gave her a confused glance.

"Why are you laughing?"

"I was picturing you slapping that bloke in the face with your superhuman strength and making him fly across the room." She laughed again. "Imagine the looks on people's faces, Jo."

Joelle grinned and Connor coughed to hide his smile, but Josh burst out laughing.

Meanwhile Joseph jumped back up to his feet.

"I will not accept this, Your Honour!" he called out. "I will appeal this decision!"

The judge smiled, while everyone else kept shaking their heads, wondering why he didn't keep his mouth shut.

"You may try Mr. Walker, but I promise you that other courts and judges will agree with the verdict. Now, with the criminal charges of sexual harassment, being an accomplice to passport forgery and supporting a human trafficking ring, I sentence you to another 10 years in prison. I now declare this trial to be over. Officers you may take Mr. Walker into custody." The judge stood up and left the room.

Two police officers handcuffed Joseph and guided him out of the building.

14. No More Judging

Ruth couldn't stop thinking about Henry Martin. She knew she had to apologise to him and thank him for watching over Hannah. She asked Hannah to look for him whenever she walked through the park on her way home from school, and to ask him to come by her office.

Unfortunately, Hannah didn't see Henry for weeks, which made Ruth feel even worse knowing it was her fault for treating him so unkind.

One afternoon, when Ruth and Hannah were both on a walk, they saw him sitting on a bench. As soon as he noticed them he wanted to disappear, but Hannah was faster.

"Henry how have you been? I've been looking for you every day the past few weeks."

"I'm doing well, Hannah, thanks." He smiled and hugged the teenager. When he looked up, Ruth smiled at him.

"Mr. Martin, may I have a word with you?" He nodded uncomfortable.

They sat on the bench when Hannah broke the silence.

"Ruth, I forgot something at home, but I'll be right back." She ran off into the direction of the cottage.

Ruth and Henry were surprised, but Hannah felt that Ruth wanted to talk to Henry alone.

"Mr. Martin, I want to apologise to you. I've wanted to apologise to you for quite some time. My behaviour towards you was rude and unpardonable and I should have never treated you the way I did."

"You're being too harsh on yourself, Mrs. Smith."

"No, Mr. Martin, I'm being honest. What I've done was wrong, and I'm so sorry." She looked at him and tried to smile. "Thank you for your kindness towards Hannah. I am so grateful that you looked after her and even put yourself in danger trying to protect her."

"That was nothing. Anyone would have done that."

"Don't be so humble. You deserve to be praised. I've been thinking about you a lot, Mr. Martin, and have concluded that I want to help you. Could you please bring me your Curriculum Vitae next time you come by?"

He smiled. "Are you going to offer me full-time employment?"

"No, but I am considering helping you open your own business."

That left him speechless.

Ruth gave him another smile. "Is there a former boss I can contact to ask about you?"

He shook his head. "I haven't had a job in years."

She raised an eyebrow.

"But you can contact my rehab clinic in Glasgow. They can tell you a lot about me."

"Great," she responded. "Please bring that information as well."

***

The next day he dropped off his CV and information about the rehab clinic. Ruth decided to drive to the clinic and meet the director of the facility herself. She asked Joelle to come with her.

The following Saturday Ruth, Joelle and Hannah drove to Glasgow.

***

It was a nice, friendly building with white bricks on the outside, a red roof, large windows and a beautiful garden. The inside looked nice as well.

Ruth, Joelle and Hannah walked toward the help desk and asked for the director. They were led into an office.

"Please have a seat." The director seated himself with the three women in front of his desk. "What can I do for you, Mrs. Smith?"

Ruth gave Joelle a quick glance. "I'm here to enquire about a former patient: Mister Henry Martin."

A big grin lit his face. "Ah, Henry." He nodded in approval and grinned again. "He's a fine man. We normally don't give personal information about our patients, but he called me and told me you might call or come by for a visit."

"What can you tell me about him? I'm wondering whether or not I should help Mister Martin start his own business as a handyman. But I don't want to invest money in a person I don't know."

The director nodded. "I understand. But you don't have to worry about Henry. When he first came to us, he didn't want to be here. Nothing we tried worked, and he didn't cooperate. One day, he changed. He never told me what happened, but since then he wanted to do everything he could to lead a normal life again. In no time he was sober, and kept working toward his goals. I've seen no one work so hard."

Joelle and Hannah smiled, both pleased. Ruth looked at them and turned back to the director.

"Did he do any work while he was here?"

"Oh yes," the director smiled. "He cooked for us. He learned quickly and enjoyed it. I was convinced he would end up as a chef one day, but he showed even more interest in fixing things. He read books about fixing everything, watched tutorials on the internet and was always teaching himself. When we discovered how good he was, we had him fix and repair things instead of hiring someone from the outside. It was cheaper that way, and it helped him improve his talents and skills."

Ruth thought for a moment.

"Do you think he could fall back into his old ways?"

"There's always a risk, but I don't think so. He's worked so hard to not let himself become discouraged since his change of heart. He's kept his optimism even with the many obstacles he's had along the way. I keep in touch with him, and he's an honest person. He's been sober for a few years now and, as far as I understand, financially he still hasn't gotten his feet back on the ground. Seems nobody wants to give him a chance due to his past." The director smiled. Ruth smiled back.

"Seriously, Mrs. Smith, if you give him the chance he deserves and needs, he will be a successful, hard working person."

Ruth thanked him for his openness and honesty and she and the others drove back to Edinburgh.

***

After driving for a while, Joelle turned to Ruth.

"What do you think?"

"I need to help, Mister Martin. I need to be willing to give him a chance and set my fears aside." She glanced in her rear view mirror and noticed that Hannah was

271

asleep. "You and Hannah were right. I misjudged him. I only saw his past and appearance and didn't want to look beyond that."

Joelle smiled. "We should be careful with strangers, but there's a voice inside each of us that tells us when it's okay to trust and believe someone."

Ruth nodded. "I know that now. You two made it clear to me."

***

Once Ruth decided to do something, she was all for it. A few days after she had been to Glasgow, she called Henry into her office.

"Mister Martin, I've decided that I want to help you start your own business. I met with the director of your rehab clinic in Glasgow and you deserve a chance."

Henry looked shocked, but smiled.

"I've prepared paperwork you must sign, but from what I've heard about you so far, I doubt you'll have any problems creating a successful business."

He smiled again. "Thank you Mrs. Smith. I don't even know how to thank you for your generosity, trust and kindness."

She blushed when he took her hand and held it looking at her in a warm, thankful way.

"It's my pleasure, Mister Martin."

***

During the next two weeks, Henry and Ruth spent a lot of time together. They bought tools and a small lorry.

She let him rent the flat she hadn't sold yet and helped him advertise his new business.

Ruth had to admit, the first time she saw him cleaned up and nicely dressed he was a fairly handsome man.

She wasn't ready yet for such feelings and pushed them aside. But his dark eyes, brown hair and strong shoulders left an impression on her.

Joelle and Josh noticed the change in Ruth, and Joelle couldn't help but praise Henry whenever possible. She had liked him from the beginning and knew he was the right person for Ruth.

It didn't take long before Henry's jobs picked up. His list of clients grew once people learned of him, his talents, fairness and honesty.

Hannah, and her friend Alissa, had gone through town to put his business cards in letter boxes, on cars and in shops advertising for him.

He saved his money to pay Ruth back, and built on his friendship with her and Hannah.

***

One night Ruth, Joelle, Hannah and Henry were sitting together in the living room at the cottage and Henry told them about his day. He had a talent for making everything sound so funny no matter how serious it was.

"This lady today was mad. Her central heating boiler wasn't working. She wanted me to fix it, but was worried I would leave dirt on her new carpet.

273

'Please be careful when you touch the heater Mister Martin,' she said. *'I want no stains or dirt on my carpet.'*

'Can you tell me how I'm supposed to fix it, if I'm not allowed to do anything?' I said back to her.

She shrugged her shoulders. *'I don't know, put something underneath it.'*

'Okay, do you have old towels I can use?' I said.

'Old towels? Shouldn't you have something?' She said.

'I haven't needed it so far. My other customers care about the thing needing fixing, not their carpets. They own hoovers you know.'"

Hannah and Ruth laughed.

"I bet she didn't appreciate that, Henry," Ruth said looking at him with a twinkle in her eyes.

"She sure didn't. She gave me a mean look, but decided not to say anything anymore. She brought me towels, and I fixed her heater. Not sure if she will call me ever again, but I couldn't handle her madness anymore."

Joelle smiled too. "And did you ruin her towels with dirt and stains?"

"I dripped water on one towel that was it."

Now turning serious, Joelle looked him straight in the eyes.

"But I have to say, it's shocking and disappointing how unprofessionally you handled the situation. How dare you talk to a paying customer in such a way! Don't you know the customer is always right?"

Stunned he looked at her, not knowing what to think about her little lecture. When he saw a cheeky little sparkle in her eyes, he nudged her arm.

"Cheeky lass, next time you scare me, I will throw you in the pool outside."

"Aren't you too old for that, Henry?" Joelle shot back.

Speechless, he gave her a warning look, but decided to teach her a lesson instead. He grabbed her by the arms and threw her over his shoulder.

"Do you still think I am too old, lass?"

Ruth and Hannah laughed again. This time it was Joelle's face that was priceless. She had not expected such a reaction.

"Okay, okay," she took herself back. "Maybe you're not that old after all. What is it with men, that whenever someone threatens their age, or manliness, they have to prove themselves by throwing someone over their shoulder?"

She gave Josh a dirty look and the guardian angels in the room laughed. Ruth and Hannah were holding their sides from laughing so hard.

Henry let Joelle off his shoulder and winked at her before giving her a hug.

"Like I said before, you are one cheeky monkey, Jo. You remind me of Taylor."

She looked up, and he smiled.

"She had the same sense of humour."

***

While Ruth and Hannah were in the kitchen doing dishes, Joelle sat next to Henry. He was a father-figure, and she knew she could talk openly with him.

"Do you miss Taylor?"

He looked at her and nodded.

"I do. I felt no romantic feelings for her, if that's what you're wondering, but she was a true friend. You're like her alright. The same cheekiness, the same directness."

She grinned picturing Taylor exactly as she was.

15. Dreadful Accident

It was a beautiful spring day at the cottage. Hannah and Ruth were hanging up laundry in the garden and Henry was on top of the roof cleaning the chimney. Birds were chirping, and it was pretty warm already considering it was just after Easter.

Joelle and Josh were standing invisible in front of the house.

Henry tried to grab one of his tools, but slipped and fell head first from the roof, not being able to stop his fall. His two guardian angels stood back.

Joelle wanted to jump in, but Josh pulled her back by the shoulders.

"We can't do anything, this is supposed to happen."

"I can't let him fall, let me go." She tried to get away from him, but he held her.

Ruth heard the loud thump, didn't see Henry on the roof anymore and ran around the house to find him lying on the ground, not moving.

"No," she whispered. "Please, no." Her face turned pale, and she knelt next to him, taking his hand into hers.

When Hannah came around the corner, she told her to call an ambulance.

Joelle turned to Josh with tears in her eyes.

"Will he die?" Josh didn't answer, just stared at the man in front of them. "JOSH," she shouted, "will he die?"

He shrugged his shoulders. "I don't know." He pulled Joelle close and hugged her until she calmed down.

The ambulance came, and they loaded Henry into the vehicle. Joelle was by his side.

"Please Henry, don't give up. Keep breathing." Tears were running down her face as she watched his guardian angels standing around motionless as if they weren't even there. "DO SOMETHING!" she shouted at them.

One of them shook his head. "There isn't anything we can do right now."

Ruth and Hannah jumped into the ambulance and a moment later it left.

It was the waiting, not knowing what was going on, that drove Ruth mad. Hannah was sitting on her chair crying. Ruth couldn't bear the thought Henry might not live through this. Finally, late in the evening, a doctor approached them.

"Are you his wife?"

Ruth shook her head, tears running down her cheeks.

"No, but we're close friends."

The doctor hesitated, but continued.

"He's not doing well. He was bleeding internally, and we had to operate. He hasn't woken yet and his heart is doing poorly. I'm not sure if he will live through the night."

Hannah cried louder. Ruth's already pale face turned as white as a bedsheet before she calmed herself.

"May we see him?" she whispered.

The doctor shook his head.

"I'm sorry, but since you're not relatives, I can't let you in. He is in the intensive-care unit and only close family members are allowed."

"We have to be with him. We're all he has."

"I'm sorry," he said and left.

***

It was past midnight and Hannah had fallen asleep. Ruth's heart felt broken. She had to be with him.

Joelle and Josh went to the ICU.

"Please, let Ruth and Hannah in," Joelle said to one of the special angels. "I know you have your rules, but they're almost family. Henry would wish for them to be with him."

The angel looked to another angel and nodded.

"Okay, we'll distract the nurses on watch," he said.

"How can we get Ruth into the ICU?"

"I can help with that." A young angel flying down the corridor, turned to Joelle and smiled. She sent strong thoughts towards Ruth.

Go into the ICU. See him now.

Ruth looked around, but the thought repeated itself. She woke Hannah, and they walked to the ICU.

She looked around, making sure nobody was watching, and slipped inside. They put on sterile gowns and gloves and hurried down the corridor looking for Henry. They found him in the last room.

Hannah cried again as soon as she saw him. Wires travelled everywhere to monitor his body functions, and he had tubes over his arms and IV's in both hands. He looked nearly dead and his heart rate was irregular.

Ruth couldn't stop looking at his face, hoping for a sign of life.

During these past months, she had become good friends with him, and close. Seeing him like this was more than she could bear.

Tears were streaming down her face and she took one of his hands in hers. Hannah stood back. Seeing him in this condition brought back memories of her parents after their accident:

It was a December night, and the roads were icy and difficult to navigate. Hannah was sitting in the middle of the backseat between her mum and her mum's friend.

280

Her dad was driving carefully, when a large lorry next to them lost control, slammed into their car and pushed them into a bridge post. Her mother had thrown herself on top of Hannah to protect her as much as possible.

When Hannah woke later, she was injured but not badly. Her mum and her parents' friends had died in the accident, but her dad was still alive.

She remembered how she walked through the hospital, and into the ICU, to watch him die a few minutes later.

***

Joelle stood next to Henry. The other guardian angels in the room, tried to leave a peaceful feeling for Ruth and Hannah, but both were too upset and sad to be comforted.

"Henry, please don't give up. Ruth and Hannah need you and you need them."

One of Henry's guardian angels touched her arm.

"Jo, there isn't anything we can do. It's not in our hands anymore."

Joelle looked at Josh and he nodded. She wiped her tears away and looked at Ruth.

Ruth was still at Henry's side holding his hand. His breathing became irregular, and she leaned forward, tears streaming down her face.

"Henry, please stay with us if you can. You mean everything to Hannah and me. I can't bear to lose you. I love you. I've never told you, but I lost a man I loved, and I don't want it to happen again. Please don't leave."

Hannah stepped closer putting her arms around Ruth and both hugged each other, sobbing. Henry Martin had stolen their hearts, and they didn't want to lose him again.

Joelle watched the heart break, leaning against Josh. He had his arms wrapped around her, trying to calm her down.

Suddenly the heart monitor flat lined, and the beeping changed to a steady tone.

Ruth jumped up. "No, please, no!"

Doctors and nurses ran into the room, Ruth, and Hannah stepped aside, watching the medical staff do what they could to revive him.

The guardian angels stood still when Henry's spirit left his body. Joelle's eyes were filled with tears.

Henry looked around, noticing Joelle.

"Jo, you're an angel?" Henry asked.

She nodded. "Yes, I'm Hannah's guardian angel."

"Why can we see you?"

"Guardian angels can make themselves invisible or visible as needed."

He turned around looking at Ruth and Hannah, at his lifeless body and the doctors and nurses working on it. He noticed the other angels and looked at Joelle again.

"Does that mean I'm dead?" He looked worried and Joelle nodded with tears in her eyes.

"So, was Taylor...."

"Yes, she used to be your guardian angel, Henry." Joelle smiled.

One of Henry's guardian angels stepped closer, addressing him with a smile and a soft voice.

"Henry," she said. "It isn't time for you to go yet. You still have things to do on this earth."

"Like marrying Ruth and adopting Hannah?"

The angels smiled and the one who just addressed him nodded.

He turned back to Joelle.

"Will I remember this once I'm back in my body?"

She shook her head. "No, you'll forget everything. You might feel really close to me, but you won't remember that I'm a guardian angel."

He smiled at her.

Josh knelt in front of Hannah, looking into her eyes, calming her down. She stopped crying, feeling as if everything would be okay.

She looked at Ruth.

"Ruth, don't cry. Everything will be all right."

Ruth hugged her more tightly, her eyes still glued to the doctors and nurses trying to bring Henry back to life.

"It's time, Henry," his angel whispered. "You need to go back to your body."

Henry smiled at each of the angels and they smiled back at him. He stepped towards Joelle to give her a hug, but she shook her head.

"Sorry Henry, but you can't hug me right now. You can only touch me as a human or after you've gone to heaven."

He smiled again and entered his body. The heart rate monitor beeped again as his heart came back to life.

Ruth let out a sigh of relief.

One nurse turned to her and Hannah. She wanted to rebuke them for being in the room, but one of Ruth's angels stared into the nurse's eyes making her forget everything she was about to say.

The nurse felt confused. She later left the room when the rest of the staff left. A few minutes later the same nurse returned bringing a second chair for Ruth.

***

"So why didn't you tell me he would make it? Are you trying to give me a heart attack?"

Josh grinned, and the other angels in the room smiled.

"No of course not. I didn't know. Besides you're already dead, so a heart attack wouldn't matter," he joked which made the angels smile again.

"None of us knew, Jo. It wasn't until after his spirit had left his body that I received the message he still had things to do," one of Henry's guardian angels responded.

"But why didn't you know? Don't we as angels know everything that will happen to the humans we protect?"

"Not exactly, no. Sometimes we know in advance what will happen. Other times, like today, we only know we shouldn't do anything and aren't certain about the outcome of the situation."

"But why?" Joelle was confused.

The angel looked at her with a smile.

"God is the only one who knows when someone's time is up. Sometimes he wants us not to interfere, even though it's hard for us to watch a human die after we've protected them for so long. Here he wanted to test Ruth to see if she was strong enough to admit that she loved Henry, and was ready to start a life with him."

That made sense, and Joelle smiled now too. She thought she had learned everything about being a guardian angel, but obviously she hadn't.

16. Friendship Often Ends in Love

When Ruth woke up the next morning, she realised she was still in Henry's room. Every muscle and bone in her body ached from spending the night in a chair.

Hannah was still asleep.

Ruth stretched, trying to get rid of the pains when Henry opened his eyes.

"Ruth," he mumbled. "What happened?"

"Henry, how are you feeling?"

"Like I got hit by a train," he tried to joke.

She smiled. "You fell off the roof, and we nearly lost you last night." She gave him a worried look. He took her hand and closed his eyes again.

Henry woke again a few hours later. A doctor came in to check on him. Ruth and Hannah left the room, but came back in later on. Henry was wide awake now and smiled at them both.

"I'm sorry I scared you two so much. I didn't mean to, I promise." He winked at Hannah and she smiled.

Ruth sat next to him and he looked into her eyes.

"I recall little of last night, but I remember you talking to me." Ruth blushed a little.

He took her hand.

"I love you too, Ruth. And I have ever since I met you. I didn't think you would ever have the same feelings for me, especially after dating Joseph and getting engaged. But when I heard your words last night, you made me the happiest man on earth."

She smiled and leaned forward to kiss his forehead.

Ruth and Hannah slept at home that night. Both felt happy and were able to get the sleep they needed after hours of worrying.

***

It was dark when Joelle and Josh walked home to the agency. Joelle felt happy and relieved that things had turned out so well.

She was completely lost in her thoughts when she heard the screeching of car tyres and a loud crash. Josh and Joelle turned around.

A car had lost control and ran full speed into a wall. The car ricocheted back into the street and got hit by a bus. There were two young women in the car. One of them was slumped over the steering wheel.

Joelle wanted to jump in and help, but Josh shook his head.

Four guardian angels were around the car. People who had witnessed the accident came to help. They heard sirens somewhere in the distance and everyone was in shock.

"What happened?" Joelle looked at Jade and Crystal who stood across from them. Both looked sad.

"The girl we've been protecting these past months, used her mobile phone while driving."

Shocked Joelle looked at Josh. They watched how the girl's spirit left her body and the car. She had a surprised expression on her face, like she couldn't believe what had happened, and disappeared.

"What will happen to the other girl?"

"She will die too," Josh replied.

People in the bus were hurt. The police, fire brigade, and ambulance arrived and tried to get the girls out of the vehicle.

As the emergency workers tried to cut the passenger out of the car, Joelle watched the second girl's spirit leave her body. With a confused look she saw the guardian angels around her, not understanding what was happening to her. Her guardian angels gave her a reassuring smile, and she too was gone.

"That's how I felt when I died. When I saw the bright light and went to heaven, I couldn't believe I was dead. Everyone was happy to see me, and yet I didn't want to be there. I thought there had been a mistake."

Josh put his arm around her shoulders pulling her close.

"That's how people feel when they've been pulled out of life before they were ready to leave. When I died, I had been sick with cancer for so long that I wanted to die and feel normal again."

Joelle nodded. She looked back at Jade and Crystal. Crystal cried and Jade tried to comfort her.

"What will happen to them now?"

"They'll receive a new assignment and will get transferred tomorrow."

Joelle didn't want to think about it. Things changed so fast. Some of her friends were leaving, or had left, and she had only a little over a month left.

Her year of training was almost over. She would have to leave Edinburgh, Josh, Hannah, Ruth and Henry.

What did she have to look forward to after this? Would she be able to tolerate and love her new partner? What was her new assignment going to be?

***

Stepping into the guardian angel office the next morning, Joelle saw several angels saying goodbye to Jade and Crystal. Crystal was in tears again, standing off to the side by herself.

Joelle jumped next to her. Giving her a warm hug, she tried to make her feel better.

"Don't be so sad, Crystal. We're all leaving soon."

Crystal sighed. "I'm not crying because of me having to leave. I still feel terrible about the accident yesterday. Maybe I could have done something...."

"Don't be so hard on yourself. You protected the girl as long as possible, but yesterday her time was up."

Crystal nodded, still sobbing.

"I'm sure my guardian angels felt the same way you do when I died. Protecting me for so long and having to let go couldn't have been easy. Trust me, it breaks my heart to think about leaving Hannah. I don't want to do it, but I know it has to happen."

"I can't help but wonder if I could have influenced our girl to not use her mobile phone while driving."

"It was her decision, and she has to deal with that now. I'm sure it will be hard for her to know she not only killed herself but her friend too."

"You're right, Jo. I wish my time here didn't have to end like this."

Together they watched Jade hug everyone.

Crystal wiped away her tears and turned to Joelle.

"Thank you, Jo."

"No problem, Crystal."

"I'll be thinking about you next month when it's your turn to leave."

"Thank you. I'm sure I'll need the support. I will miss Hannah so much."

"… and Josh," Crystal added not looking at Joelle.

Jo turned to her, but didn't know what to say. She blushed and noticed a smile on Crystal's face. Before she could say anything, someone grabbed her hands and pulled her into his arms.

"Connor, are you leaving, as well?" She looked up to him and he gave her warm smile.

"Yes. I am being transferred to Utah."

"Are you going to be an undercover cop again?"

"No, but I will look after a police officer. Jo, before I go I want to apologise one more time. I am still so sorry about how much I scared you during the situation with Joseph Walker. At the same time I am so glad we met. You are an incredible, strong and beautiful woman and I will miss seeing you."

Joelle smiled, but blushed by his words.

"I will miss seeing you, too. And don't worry about the Joseph Walker situation. That is all forgotten." She winked at him and he grinned while wiping hair out of her face.

Jade reached out to Joelle and hugged her.

"Cheerio my friend, until we will meet again," Jade said.

"Where are you going?"

"I'm being sent to Australia this time. I'll be in charge of a wee blind boy. It will be a completely new challenge."

Crystal now hugged Joelle as well.

"I'll be serving as an angel in a retirement home in Norway."

She smiled again and everyone stepped back. Jade and Crystal snapped their fingers, and they were gone.

Before Connor snapped his fingers though, he pulled Joelle tight into his arms.

"I am in love with you, Jo!" he whispered into her ear, stepped back, snapped his fingers and disappeared.

Jo was in shock when she watched him leave. Her whole human life had she dreamed of someone saying those words to her, and it never happened.

Maybe there was a reason for it? Perhaps meeting someone on earth, had not been part of her plan. Maybe the right person had not been around her at that time.

She had to admit, she had a crush on Connor. Not only was he tall and handsome, but she loved his personality and sense of humour. She knew in her heart she could be happy with him. Time would tell what the future had in store for her, and whether or not Connor was meant for her.

***

Ruth took Hannah to school that morning and went back to the hospital.

Henry was awake and watched her as she walked into the room. He looked much better and his face lit up as soon as he saw her.

"Ruth," was all he said.

She smiled too and touched his arm.

Ruth, when I'm better and get out of the hospital, will you marry me?" He looked at her, wondering if he had asked to soon, before she was ready for it.

She gasped for a moment, not knowing what to say.

Am I ready to take this step? Do I love him enough to marry him right now?

Her heart told her yes. She knew it was the right thing to do. She knew she loved him, that he would make her happy, and that he loved Hannah as much as she did.

"Yes," she said smiling at him. "I will marry you."

A huge grin appeared on his face. Since he couldn't move much, Ruth leaned forward and kissed him on the lips.

***

When Hannah arrived at the hospital in the afternoon, Ruth and Henry greeted her with a grin.

"Why are you smiling like that? Did I miss something?"

Ruth nodded. "Henry proposed." A big happy smile appeared on Ruth's face. Hannah looked from one to the other and flew into Ruth's open arms.

"I'm so happy for you both."

Joelle walked in at that moment. She had heard the news, but pretended she had no idea.

Hannah jumped up and into Joelle's arms.

"Guess what, Jo. Henry and Ruth are getting married. I will have a real family again." She smiled and Joelle held her.

"Congratulations, you two. That was quick considering a few days ago you two weren't even dating." There was a cheeky sparkle in her eyes and Henry wondered what was going on in her mind.

He felt close to Joelle, closer than ever, but didn't know why. Joelle smiled. She knew and sometime in the future he would remember, too.

"Jo," he said, "what's going on in that pretty head of yours?"

She grinned. "It's nothing."

"You can't fool me, lass. If I wasn't stuck to this bed because I can't move, I would get up and make you tell me." His eyes were glued to her face as if he tried to burn a hole in her head to find out what she thought.

She grinned again. "I bet you would."

Ruth stared at her now too.

"I just remembered the day I first met you, Henry," she said simply.

"And?" he asked her.

"And my first thought was that you would be perfect for Ruth."

"No way." Ruth's jaw dropped in disbelief. "Don't tell me that your agency told you to find a husband for me too."

Joelle laughed out loud. "No of course not, I was looking after Hannah, but I couldn't help my female matchmaking tendencies."

Josh and the other guardian angels burst out laughing. Henry grinned from ear to ear, and after a while Ruth had a big smile on her face too.

"You're an interesting person, Jo."

Henry looked Joelle directly in her eyes.

"Maybe she's a wizard and put a spell on us."

With no one noticing she winced. She felt Josh's hands on her shoulders and had to be careful with her response.

Can he remember the night when his spirit left his body? She thought.

"No he can't. He senses a special closeness to you, but he remembers nothing," one of Henry's guardian angels reassured her.

But why did he say that? Are you sure he can't remember?

"He's playing with you. He remembers nothing. I'm sure." Josh stood in front of her now, giving her the calming stare.

"See, she's a wizard. She's gone off into her own little world now." Henry smiled at her, but this time Joelle had her response ready.

"Yes, you're right, Henry. I was thinking of a spell to turn you into a toad."

Ruth and Hannah laughed and Henry grinned again. He winked at her and she knew there was no chance he would remember.

***

The next few weeks went by fast. Ruth prepared everything for Hannah's adoption. She met with the orphanage, contacted Hannah's lawyer in London and set things up that after she and Henry were married, they would both be able to make the adoption official.

Hannah was over the moon with excitement. After months of being by herself, running away repeatedly and missing her parents, she felt like her life had become normal once more and worth living!

Henry recovered well too. He healed fast and was released within a fortnight. He had to take it easy and wasn't allowed to go right back to work. (Ruth didn't want him on a roof again anytime soon.) He gave himself lots of rest and cooked for his two girls every night.

***

When Ruth's colleagues heard of her engagement to a handyman, they badmouthed him until Ruth exploded.

"You have no right to judge him or say anything bad about him. He's a wonderful man and I love him with all my heart. I don't care if he's a handyman or even a farmer or a lawyer. He doesn't have to have a better profession than I do. We're right for each other, and that's what matters. Either be happy for me or leave me alone."

That did the trick, and nobody said anything ever again. But rather than being offended, they had to admit they respected her even more.

***

One warm evening in May, a few days before the wedding, Henry and Ruth went for a walk in the park.

After minutes of silence, Ruth turned to him.

"Henry, thank you for loving me the way I am."

He pulled her into his strong arms and kissed her.

"I can't help it, Ruth. You're the one for me."

"Well, I wasn't kind to you in the beginning. I misjudged you. I was cold and reserved, and wouldn't have ever changed my mind about you if it wasn't for Hannah and Joelle."

He smiled, brushing her hair behind her ear.

"But you listened to Hannah and Joelle. We all judge in one way or another. That you were willing to change, and get to know the real me, shows me what a wonderful person you are. I love you, Ruth, and that will never change."

She kissed him on his cheek and smiled.

"And you're okay with us adopting Hannah?"

He pulled her even closer. "Yes. I love Hannah. She is one special lass. She trusted and accepted me from the beginning. We wouldn't be the family we are now if it wasn't for her."

The big day arrived. It was a small, intimate wedding, and everyone that had been invited came.

Hannah couldn't have been happier. After the "I do's" and kiss, she jumped up and ran into Henry's arms, hugging him tightly. Ruth had tears in her eyes when she saw their warm embrace.

Only two days later they went to the orphanage and signed the papers, making Hannah their daughter.

Joelle had tears streaming down her face as she hugged Hannah.

"You have a real family now," she whispered into Hannah's ear.

"Yes thank you, Jo, all because of you."

Joelle held her in her arms and was very grateful.

17. Time to Say Goodbye

As much as Joelle dreaded this day, it came, and she had to face leaving whether or not she liked it. Josh tried to cheer her up as much as possible, but she couldn't help the sad feeling, leaving those she loved.

It was a beautiful and warm Sunday in Edinburgh. After church, Henry, Ruth and Hannah spent the day with Josh and Joelle playing games, enjoying each other's company, talking and having a barbecue.

Joelle didn't want the day to end, but as the sun went down, she couldn't postpone it any longer.

Josh knew how she felt. He too didn't feel like leaving, but it was time.

Henry and Ruth felt that something had been bothering Joelle for the past few days. They were sitting in the living room when Joelle broke the silence.

"I have something to tell you."

Everyone looked at her, but the sad look on her face told them it wasn't something pleasant.

Josh moved closer to her and grabbed her hand.

"Our agency will send us somewhere else."

Hannah couldn't believe her ears. "What?"

"We're leaving," Joelle said.

Henry pressed Ruth closer to him.

"When do you have to leave?"

"Tomorrow."

Hannah, still in shock, looked from Josh to Joelle.

Ruth stood up and walked to Joelle, giving her a hug.

"We will miss you."

"I will miss you too." Still trying to hold back her tears she looked at Ruth.

Hannah jumped up from the couch.

"But you can't leave, Jo. This isn't fair." She ran out of the room.

Swallowing her tears, Joelle followed Hannah. She found her outside, next to the pool, hands in front of her face, crying. Joelle pulled back Hannah's hands and Hannah turned around and threw her arms around Joelle's neck, holding her tight.

"You can't leave, Jo. You're my friend. You were there for me when I needed someone the most, and I love you."

Joelle couldn't help it and cried too. She had fought back her tears for so long, but hearing those three words out of Hannah's mouth did it. She pulled the girl closer, and they sobbed together.

"I will miss you too, Hannah, believe me I will."

"This isn't fair. Why can't they leave you here and send someone else?"

"I have more things to do, Hannah. I've accomplished what I had to do here, finding you a new home and family. Now I'm needed somewhere else."

"Will I see you again?"

"Someday."

She held Hannah in her arms until she heard Ruth, Henry and Josh come outside. Only then did she remove Hannah's arms and stood up.

Ruth had now tears in her eyes too. Henry smiled a sad smile and more tears appeared in Joelle's eyes.

Without thinking about it, Henry walked over to Joelle and pulled her into his arms. She leaned against him, sobbing and feeling heartbroken.

"We will never forget you, Jo. Thank you for taking care of Hannah, and bringing us together. We love you."

He kissed her head. It was like holding an older daughter and hard for him to see her leave.

Josh, knowing he had to make this easier for everyone, touched Joelle's hand.

"We have to go, Jo."

She nodded and hugged Henry one last time.

"Please watch over Ruth and Hannah," she whispered.

"I will, I promise."

She gave Ruth another hug and said her final farewell to Hannah.

"I love you, Hannah, and I will never forget you."

She turned around and without looking back left the garden.

***

Back in the park Josh and Joelle made themselves invisible as soon as nobody was around.

Joelle was still in tears. Josh pulled her into his arms, trying to comfort her as much as possible, but it didn't help much. She still had to say goodbye to him.

"Will this ever get easier?" she asked him with tears running down her cheeks.

He kissed her forehead. "I wish I could answer that with a yes, but I can't. It's always hard to leave a place, the people we've watched over for so long, and the angels we've served with," he said looking in her eyes.

"But why do we have to move on? Can't we stay with one person?"

"Do you think that would make it easier in the end? No. Besides, we have different skills and talents needed by different humans. It's something we have to endure. And don't forget we will see them again."

She sighed, calming down.

They walked through Edinburgh one last time and headed back to headquarters.

"This is so not cool," she couldn't help saying out loud. "I don't want to leave."

"I know. But it's hard for everyone, even the angels who work in heaven."

"Really?"

He nodded. "They cope with it better, because they see everyone more often, but it's still hard. Taylor was very sad when she had to leave you with me."

"Wow I had no idea."

"Yes that was the first time I've seen her upset over something like that."

Joelle couldn't believe it. *So it isn't just me who feels that way?* "What will happen tomorrow morning?" She didn't want to think about it, but had to know.

"I'll leave for my new destination and assignment, and you'll be picked up and taken to your new destination."

"Why can't I go alone?"

"It's this last time."

"Will Taylor come and pick me up?"

"No she was transferred somewhere else. Sydney took her job."

A little smile appeared on her face. At least someone she knew.

They arrived at the office and said a quick good night to each other. Both didn't want to think about the next morning.

Departure day for Josh and Joelle. Joelle was in tears, saying goodbye to everyone that came for her last farewell. She kept thinking about her friends that had left during the last few weeks.

She thought about Henry, Ruth and Hannah and having to say goodbye to Josh in a few minutes. Sydney appeared, and it was time.

Josh forced himself through the crowd and looked into her eyes.

"Where are you going, Josh?"

"I'm going to Canada. I'll be living in Toronto, working with a young drug addict."

She nodded, tears running down her face as she threw herself into his arms one last time. He held her tight.

"We'll see each other again, Jo. It's not a farewell forever."

"I know, but I will miss you so much, Josh."

He pulled her even closer.

"I'll miss you too, Jo, more than you can imagine."

He stepped away from her and she looked at him one last time. Sydney snapped her fingers, and they both disappeared into nothingness.

As they travelled further and further away from Edinburgh, Joelle forced herself to look forward, not back. Many new things were waiting for her: new assignments, new challenges, and new possibilities to make someone's life better and happier.

About the Author

Rebecca was born and raised in Germany and lived there until 2002 when she served a mission for her church in Scotland. She is a member of the Church of Jesus Christ of Latter-day Saints and has been living in the United States since 2004. She and her husband have two boys.

Rebecca has been writing stories since her teenage years, and decided in the summer of 2012 to become more serious about it. This book is the first of the "Heavenly Bodyguards" trilogy. In February of 2013, Rebecca published a little cookbook, and is currently working on writing her fourth book.

Dictionary: British English/ Scottish – American English

189 meters	-	620 ft
230 meters	-	755 ft
Blether	-	holding a conversation
blimey	-	expression of surprise
block of flats	-	apartment building
bloke	-	guy
brilliant	-	amazing
bum	-	butt
central heating boiler	-	furnace; heating system
chat-up line	-	pick up line
cheeky	-	sassy
cheerio	-	bye
corridor	-	hall way
Curriculum Vitae; CV	-	resume
custard	-	vanilla pudding (sort of)
dimwit	-	idiot; bonehead
dodgy	-	creepy

dosser	-	lazy person; tramp
fetch	-	get someone
fire brigade	-	fire department
flat	-	apartment
fortnight	-	two weeks; 14 days
Garden	-	backyard
gash	-	wound
git	-	scumbag
gran/ granny	-	Grandma
granddad	-	Grandpa
Haggis	-	*A sausage made from the minced heart, liver and lungs of a sheep mixed with oatmeal, suet, minced onion, spices, herbs and seasoning, all encased in a sheep's stomach and boiled prior to being served hot.*
halfwit	-	jerk
hammered	-	wasted
hasty	-	fast
headmaster	-	principal

Dictionary: British English/ Scottish – American English

holidays	-	vacation; school break
Honour	-	Honor
hoover	-	vacuum
jumper	-	sweater/ sweatshirt
knackered	-	exhausted
lads	-	boys
lass	-	girl
letter box	-	mail box
lorry	-	truck
mad	-	crazy
mobile phone	-	cell phone
motorway	-	freeway
mum	-	mom
Neeps	-	turnip
Oi	-	Hey
operation	-	surgery
pavement	-	sidewalk

plaster	-	band aid
pound	-	prison; jail
rubbish	-	garbage
shop	-	store
Stone the crows	-	Holy cow
straight away	-	immediately
supper	-	dinner
Tatties	-	potatoes
Trousers	-	pants
wee	-	little
tosser	-	jerk/ idiot

Scottish sayings:

Aye, juist a wee bit	-	Yes, a little bit.
Can A gie ye a haund?	-	What can I do for you?
D'ye spaek Scots	-	Do you speak Scottish?
Guid mornin!	-	Good morning
Ho ye!	-	Just a moment.
Nice tae meit ye!	-	Nice to meet you!
Whaur ar ye frae?	-	Where are you from?

Heavenly Bodyguards - Against all Evil

"Tell me something Bri, has giving up made you happy? Has your situation changed because you feel sorry for yourself? How can you expect others to stop feeling sorry for you, if you're not willing to stop feeling sorry for yourself?"

Convincing a healthy, beautiful teenage girl to believe in herself is hard, but the task becomes almost impossible when seventeen-year-old Brianna has an accident that will change her life forever. Joelle's task is to help Brianna understand that she needs to love herself no matter what, and giving up hope isn't an option - life is still beautiful.

But this isn't her only mission. Joelle receives two more assignments - even more demanding and intense. Abuse, bullying and racism are some challenges that await her. However, things finally look up for her when, for the second time, she discovers a power none of the other angels seem to have.

Made in the USA
Lexington, KY
09 November 2019

56799404R00179